To Glori
wonderf

Carol A. Baker

nancy Baker-Dansby

Brick Walls: The Sheriff

Carl A. Baker
&
Nancy Baker-Dansby

authorHOUSE®

AuthorHouse™
1663 Liberty Drive
Bloomington, IN 47403
www.authorhouse.com
Phone: 1 (800) 839-8640

Published by AuthorHouse 02/07/2017

ISBN: 978-1-5246-6987-4 (sc)
ISBN: 978-1-5246-6988-1 (e)

ACKNOWLEDGEMENT

As you have noticed, I have a co-author on this book, Nancy Baker-Dansby, who is an author in her own right. She has been very helpful with this book and made great contributions to its completion. We have enjoyed co-authoring and may do another book in the near future.

I hope you have enjoyed Brick Walls: The Sheriff as much as the first edition of Brick Walls. It has been a great satisfaction to complete it.

CHAPTER ONE

The hot Texas sun was slowly rising in the east over the county of Medina. Brick's old white truck was kicking up dust as he drove down the dirt road toward his property in the country. He stopped the truck as he came to the fence. "Stay in here, boy," he said to his Irish setter, who was excitedly waiting to explore the field. Brick opened the gate, got back in the truck and pulled onto the property. He stopped the truck, walked around to the other side and opened the door. "Alright, Red, you can go run and get some exercise. Go, boy!" Red pushed past him, jumped out of the truck and went running through the grass looking for rabbits or birds or anything else he could find. Red was truly enjoying himself, and Brick laughed out loud as he watched the dog running and hunting out in the field.

Brick walked back to the gate to close it, and then meandered on down along the fence a short distance. He looked at the property on the other side of the fence. It had a large burned-out area in the middle of the field where over a year ago a private plane had crashed and caught fire. There was another burn spot where a truck had blown up during the same incident. His thoughts went back to the events that caused this to happen. "How did I ever get myself mixed up in all of that?" Brick shook his head as he watched Red chase a squirrel. The truth of the matter was, he got involved because his Irish setter grabbed the money bag that was a part of a drug deal which ended in flames and murder.

Brick started thinking about the wonderful people he had met during the past year, and how they helped him fend off the ex-sheriff turned drug dealer who was stalking him. He was staring out at the dry land before him, when he dropped his head as tears started filling his light blue eyes. "Oh Helen," he whispered aloud. Never, had he been so in love with someone as he was with Helen. He longed to be able to turn back the hands of time, so he could have rescued Helen before the drug dealer killed her. He remembered holding her lifeless body after she whispered, "I love you," with her dying breath. Brick wondered if he would ever find another woman to love as much as he loved Helen. He wasn't sure he would even want to try.

His thoughts were reminders that no one ever knows what the future holds. And little did Brick know that he would once again face unexpected danger, because of the money that Red found in this field a year ago.

Brick also thought about the events that followed after he came back to Maranda. It was only eight months ago when he decided to run for sheriff and was elected. He was honored to protect the people of his county, and it felt good to be back in his home town with a purpose in his life.

Brick smiled and looked up at the sky just in time to see a red-tailed hawk circling above him, looking for rodents or anything else it could eat in the field below. The hawk majestically rode the thermals with almost no effort as it searched for its next meal, paying little or no attention to Brick or Red. Just then, Red came galloping up and barked. He wanted Brick to come out into the field with him. Brick looked at his watch and realized he had better get Red back in the truck and head to work. It was Wednesday morning, and he had some papers to get ready for the court.

"Come on, Red, let's get back in the truck. You've had your exercise for the day. I think you've run all over my forty-four acres here. You should be tired out by now." Red reluctantly followed Brick back to the truck and jumped up into the front seat. Brick went to unlock the gate, backed out, closed the gate and locked it. There wasn't anything on the property for anyone to steal, but it was good to keep the property safe. No telling what someone might do to damage or burn it. He pulled out onto the dirt road and headed back to town.

As he drove along, he thought about the people he hired for the sheriff's department. There were four deputies: Billy Roy Bryant, George Kimbell, Sam Akins, and Albert Watkins. Billy Roy was new to the business and had just graduated from the police academy. He didn't seem to be a "sharp tack", and Brick felt like it might take a while before Billy Roy got the "hang" of the job.

George Kimbell came down from Michigan, because he wanted to get out of the cold weather. He had several years experience in the law enforcement field, and Brick thought he would be a great addition to the department. George and his wife, Gloria, both loved Texas now and wanted to start a family in the Lone Star State.

Sam Akins had been a deputy under the previous sheriff, but had resigned because of the questionable activities of Sheriff Mendez. Brick was very happy to have Sam back on the department, and Sam was eager to work for an honest sheriff. His familiarity with the county area and the department's assets were an immediate help to Brick.

Albert Watkins was a long-time resident of the county who had been working for the Maranda Police Department for four years and had answered Brick's ad in the local paper for an experienced law enforcement officer. Albert wanted to be a detective and felt like he had too much seniority competition on the police department to achieve his goal, so he decided to go to work for the new sheriff.

Each deputy worked a 10-hour day. Brick put Billy Roy on the day shift where he could keep a close eye on him, assigned George to begin work at mid-morning to help on both day and evening shift, and put Albert on the evening/late night shift so that he could continue his classes in police science at the local junior college.

Sam agreed to cover the other deputies' days off, with the understanding that, as the department grew, he would be in line to become Chief Deputy.

In addition to the deputies, Brick also hired two ladies for the office: Bonnie Lumpkin and Juanita Hemstead. Bonnie spent three years in the army working as a military police dispatcher and had some law enforcement experience as well. Brick felt like she was a good candidate, but she just had to get over the habit of saluting and calling him, "Sir."

He remembered the day she came in for her interview. She had just come through the front door, so he called her into his office. She walked in, snapped to attention, and said "Yes, Sir!"

"Well ma'am it's not necessary for you to salute me. We don't have that kind of regimentation here. You can just relax a little."

"Yes, Sir, I will do so....Sir." She sat down in the chair in front of his desk.

After reading her resume and listening to her during the interview, Brick said, "Well, Bonnie, I think you might fit in real well."

"Thank you, Sir. I appreciate it, Sir!"

"Ah, Bonnie, please don't call me "Sir" every time. My name is Brick or you can just call me Sheriff."

"Yes, Sir, Sheriff...oh I'm sorry, Sir....it's just a habit, Sir."

"Well," he chuckled, "that's OK. How about reporting the day after tomorrow, and I'll have your office ready for you?"

"Thank you, Sir, very much." She almost snapped to attention, then stopped herself.

Brick laughed and said, "Old habits are hard to break aren't they? I'll see you day after tomorrow at eight o'clock sharp." She smiled, turned around, and left the office as if she were marching. Brick just shook his head and chuckled.

Shortly after Bonnie left, his other office candidate arrived. Juanita was nineteen years old and didn't have the experience that Brick really wanted, but seemed eager to work for Brick. She made it quite clear during the interview that she really needed a job.

As he looked over her resume, she said with lots of enthusiasm, "Sheriff, I know I don't have any law enforcement experience, but I really would like to work for you, and I think I'd do really well for you in this job." She continued, "I've worked in an office before, and I make coffee that is out of this world. It'll turn you "loose as a goose".

Brick replied, "Well, I'm not sure that's exactly what I wanted, but I…" He changed the subject quickly. "You live here in town, right?"

"Yes, Sir. I live with my mama. My daddy done left us a bunch of years ago, but you know that's OK, 'cause I don't care. He didn't want us, and we didn't want him."

Brick said, "Well, that's one way to look at it, Juanita."

"Yeah, my mama said good riddance to bad stuff, ya know?"

Brick put down the resume and thought for a second. She seemed to be a nice lady. "Ah, well, I'll tell you what I'm gonna do, I'm gonna give you a chance to learn the job. You seem to be a bright person, and I think maybe we'll get along real well."

Juanita jumped up out of her seat almost shouting, "Great, Sheriff!! Can I start the job today…this afternoon?"

"Ah, not this afternoon. Be here the day after tomorrow at eight, and we'll start training you. I'll go over some things, and you'll meet the rest of the people. You'll also meet Bonnie who will be working with you in the office."

Juanita interrupted Brick. "Oh boy, I've got friends, huh?"

Brick was beginning to wonder if he made the right decision due to her overzealous response. "Yes, you'll have friends."

"Oh good, I like people. I like to talk."

"Now, there won't be a lot of talking. You'll have work to do."

"Yes, but I'll be talking on the phone, won't I?"

Brick nodded his head. "Now I'll see you the day after tomorrow."

"Oh thank you so much, Sheriff!" She was very excited as she left the office. It looked like he had made her day. Brick smiled. He took her on with reservations that if she couldn't handle the job, he would have to let her go. So far, he thought, everything was working out just fine.

Brick made the turn and pulled into the parking lot. "Another day at the office," he smiled as he and Red got out of the truck and walked into the building. He was pleased that everything seemed to be going well at the office. Both of the ladies proved to be capable. The deputies had proven to be reliable and professional, as well. Everything seemed to be settling down in pretty good shape. Brick smiled and went into his office.

The phone in his office started to ring. Brick picked it up, "Sheriff Walls."

"Hi, Sheriff, this is Bob."

"Hi, Bob, how ya doing?" Bob was the local veterinarian and a long time friend of Brick's.

"Are you busy, Sheriff?"

"Well, not right at this moment. I was just having a cup of coffee. Why don't you come over and have a cup with me."

Bob seemed pleased with the invitation. "Do you mind?"

"Naw, that's fine." Brick replied.

"Ok," said Bob. "I'll be right over."

Brick hung up the phone, sat back in his chair, and took a sip of coffee. "Now, I wonder what Bob wants?" He muttered to himself.

In a little while, Bob showed up at the office. Juanita poured him a cup of coffee as he walked into Brick's office. "Good morning, my friend," said Brick as he stood and shook Bob's hand.

"Good morning," Bob said as he sat down in the visitor's chair at the front of Brick's desk. Juanita placed his cup of coffee on the desk while the men were talking.

"Now what brings you in this fine morning?"

"Well, Brick, I seem to recall that your birthday is coming up on Saturday." He took a sip of coffee.

"Hmm. You *would* have to remind me. Here I was trying to forget." They laughed.

"Well, I'm thinking we ought to have a party at my place. You can ask your fellow workers and their dates, and I'll ask a couple of our other friends. We'll start at around seven o'clock. What do you think?"

"That's really nice of you, Bob. It sounds good. What do you need me to do?"

"I need you to get yourself a date for this shindig." He looked straight at Brick as he took another sip of coffee.

"Bob, you know I'm not dating right now."

"Yes, I know, but it's time you did. There's more to life than work, Brick. Why don't you ask Sally? She seems to enjoy being around you, and I know you two dated in high school."

"Ya, we did." Brick thought about what Bob said as he took a long sip of coffee. "Ok. I'll give her a call and see if she'd like to accompany me to the party."

"Great! Well, I need to get back to the vet clinic," Bob said as he put his cup back on the desk. "How's old Red doing?"

"He's outside in the back if you'd like to go see him." Brick stood as Bob headed toward the door.

"Naw, I've got to run." He stopped and turned around back to Brick. "You know, Brick, I'm really glad you came back here and ran for sheriff. I know you'll keep this the peaceful, safe place that we all have enjoyed all of our lives." He shook Brick's hand and left.

"Thanks, Bob," Brick said as Bob closed the front office door. "That was a nice thing he just told me," Brick thought to himself. "I'm really glad I came back, too!"

He went back to his desk and took another sip of coffee. "I'll have to call Sally about going with me to the party Saturday. I hope I'm ready for this," he said to himself. Just then the phone rang, and he put aside his thoughts about a date with Sally and got back to work.

CHAPTER TWO

It was Thursday morning. Brick and Red had already gone through their regular routine of breakfast and watering Mom's Garden. While he was putting on his uniform, Brick wondered if he should go ahead and make the phone call he'd been hesitant to make.

"Am I ready for this?" He wondered. He finished getting dressed, picked up the phone and dialed the number of the Sweet Pea Café. An elderly sounding lady answered the phone.

"Sweet Pea Café, may I help you?"

"Let me talk to Sally, please."

"Ok, just a moment." Brick heard Marie, the cook, call out for Sally.

A sweet voice answered the phone, "This is Sally."

Brick took a deep breath. "Hi, Sally. This is Brick."

"Oh, hi Brick, how are you doing? Are you coming over to the café this morning?"

"Well, I'm probably gonna be on the road today, but I just wanted to see if you are doing anything Saturday night?"

"Well, what do you have in mind?" She was intrigued with what he was about to say.

"Saturday's my birthday, and they're having a party for me at Dr. Bob's place. I just thought you might like to go with me."

"Oh I'd love to Brick. What time?"

"Well, supposing I pick you up about seven o'clock."

"That would be just fine." Sally was excited. She had been hoping that they would have an opportunity to date again.

"Ok, I'll see you then."

"Thanks, Brick, for asking me."

"My pleasure, Sally. Goodbye", he said relieved that she accepted his invitation.

Brick could tell by the sound of Sally's voice that she was very happy. He put the phone down and released a big sigh of relief. "Well, now I'm committed. I don't know if it's the thing to do or not. I don't want to get involved too quickly, but she sure is a nice gal. We'll just see how it goes."

Brick dated Sally in high school. She was a sweet girl then and had grown into a beautiful and caring woman. This would be Brick's first date since Helen's death last year in Las Vegas. It was because of Helen's death that Brick left Vegas and came back home to Maranda to run for Sheriff.

CHAPTER THREE

The phone kept ringing all morning at the Sheriff's office. Brick noticed that Juanita was handling it very well. There were several calls about minor things, and people asking if the sheriff was going to be in their area soon. They wanted him to stop by and talk to them. Brick had instructed Juanita that if anyone wanted him to visit, she should tell them that he'd be glad to do just that. She was to take their name, address, and phone number, and Brick would set up an appointment with them when he was going to be in their part of the county. He didn't really enjoy this political part of being Sheriff, but it was necessary both to keep up with what was happening in the county and it also helped him at election time.

There were two calls of complaints of cattle loose in their area. Billy Roy was on another call, so Brick told Juanita to handle the fort, and he would go out to see what he could do. He got into the squad car and drove out to the location where the cattle had been reported loose. Sure enough, there were two cows out on the highway. Brick stopped and with the aid of two farmers, he was able to get them herded back into their proper location. The farmers appreciated Brick's prompt response. They shook hands and went their separate ways.

Juanita was calling him just as he was getting back into the car.

"Yes Juanita, this is the Sheriff."

"This is Juanita."

"Yes, Juanita, I know it's you", he replied rolling his eyes.

"Oh well, I just wanted to let you know that Billy Roy called in and told me where he was gonna be. He wanted me to call him back in 30 minutes, if I didn't hear from him. So I don't know what to do Sheriff." She seemed rather worried.

"Well, did he call back?" Brick was rather confused by this conversation.

"Ah, no."

"Has it been 30 minutes?"

"No," she said, wondering why he would ask her that.

"Well, when it gets to be 30 minutes, and he hasn't called, then you call him." Brick's head was slowly shaking back and forth.

"Ah, well, ok that sounds good doesn't it?"

"Yeah, well, you hang in there girl. I'll be in the office shortly," he said with a smirk.

"Ok, Sheriff, over and out!" Juanita hung up the phone.

"Yeah...over and out," Brick said to himself. "I don't know about this. I don't know if she'll work out or not, but she sure is sweet and trying hard. I guess we'll put up with her a little longer. Maybe it'll get better."

It wasn't long before he received another call. This one was from his deputy, George Kimbell.

"Ah, Sheriff?"

"Ya, George..." Brick couldn't wait to see what George had to say.

"I just wanted to check in. Everything's pretty quiet. I've had to give two speeding tickets out on the highway here. I don't know why, but a couple of kids were drag racing on the highway.

I caught them both, so I gave them speeding tickets. Was that the right thing to do?"

"Were they speeding?" Brick couldn't wait to hear the answer.

"Ya"

Rolling his eyes, Brick responded, "Well that seems to be the right thing to do. Doesn't it, George?"

"Yes, sir, just making sure you did things the same here as we did in Michigan."

"Ok, George, keep up the good work!" Brick couldn't keep himself from chuckling.

"Ok, Sheriff." They hung up.

Brick was laughing out loud by this point, "Well, at least he didn't say 'over and out'."

Brick headed back to the office. Juanita met him at the door.

"Ah, Sheriff?" She seemed a little stressed.

"Yes, Juanita," he said as he was walking into his office.

"I didn't hear from Billy Roy."

"You didn't. Well, did you call him?"

"Yes, but he didn't answer." It was obvious she was very concerned.

Brick thought a moment. "Did you call him on the car phone?"

"Yes, that's the number I called, and he didn't answer."

"Ok. How about his cell phone, did you try that?"

Juanita looked shocked that she hadn't thought of that. "Ah, no."

Brick looked her straight in the eye. "Let's try that cell phone."

"Good idea, Sheriff."

She quickly walked back into her office and proceeded to look up Billy Roy's cell phone number. She was shaking as she dialed the phone and walked back into Brick's office.

"No answer, Sheriff."

"Where did he say he was going to be?" Brick was starting to get a little concerned at this point.

"He said he would be at the four corners, and he was going off on to a little side road."

Brick decided he'd better drive out there to see what was going on. "You stay by the phone, and I'll go on out there to see if he needs some help. He's probably alright and just doesn't have his phone with him. But I'll go check on him."

Juanita looked relieved that Brick was going to look for Billy Roy. "Ok, Sheriff."

"If anything happens I'll call you," he told Juanita as he grabbed his hat and walked out the door.

Brick got back into his squad car and headed out west toward Billy Roy's area. It didn't take long to reach the Four Corners Grocery and Feed Stores. He didn't see the squad car anywhere so he pulled into the parking lot of the grocery store, got out of his car, and walked into the store.

"Hi there, Sheriff," the store owner said as he walked up to Brick to shake his hand.

"Hi, Todd. Have you seen my deputy lately?"

"Well, he was here earlier this morning. We talked awhile, and then he must have left. I got busy with some customers, and I didn't see him go. He wasn't around there later when I looked. Some of the boys were talking with him, maybe they know."

"Well I'll check. Are they over at the feed store?"

"Yeah," he said as he walked over to wait on a customer.

"Thanks." Brick walked across the parking lot to the feed store. Four workers were standing outside the store smoking.

Brick nodded his head to them. "Hi, fellas."

"Howdy, Sheriff." They shook Brick's hand.

"Have you seen my deputy today?"

"Yeah, we talked to him this morning." The men were curious why the Sheriff would be asking them about his deputy. They started getting the feeling that something may not be right.

"Do you know where he went?"

"Ah, no can't say as I do," said the man closest to Brick. He turned to one of the other men. "Hey, Charlie, did you see where the deputy went?"

"No, but he was talking to Ben. Maybe Ben knows." The men put their cigarettes out and started to return to work.

Brick continued, "Is Ben here?"

"Naw, he went on home, but I did see him talking to the deputy out there by his truck."

"Ok, do you know where Ben lives?"

"Go down to the next street and turn left. You'll see an old dirt road there. Ben's house is up there about a quarter of a mile." Charlie waved to Brick as he turned to go back to work.

Brick waved thanks, got back into the squad car and eased on down the highway. He found the dirt road, turned left and sure enough up about a quarter of a mile was a rather run down house with two scraggly looking cows in the back pasture, and an old dog sitting on the front porch. Brick eased into the driveway and stepped out of the car. The dog started a low growl, then a bark, then a low growl again. It stood up and came to the edge of the porch. Brick thought, "I don't know if I want to tangle with him or not."

"Ben," he hollered. There was no answer. The dog started the low growl again and went into a crouch. Brick kept an eye on him as he called out again, "Ben? Ben, are you there?" Brick was relieved when he heard a male voice calling out.

"Just a minute! Just a minute!" The front door opened. The dog sat back and looked up at Ben. Ben said, "It's alright just sit down....down!" The dog laid back down, but he kept his eye on Brick.

"What cha need, Sheriff?" said Ben as he extended his hand to shake Brick's. Ben was in great shape for a man in his mid sixties. His face had very few wrinkles, and his hair was just starting to get hints of gray. It was evident he did a lot of physical work which kept his six foot frame very muscular.

"Hi, Ben. How ya doing?"

"Just great, Sheriff. What brings you up here?"

"I was just wondering, do you know where my deputy went today? The boys at the feed store said they saw you talking to him, and we haven't heard from him since."

"Ah, shit!" Ben looked irritated.

Brick didn't like the look on Ben's face. "What's the matter?"

"Um, I may have got him into some trouble."

"How's that?" Brick was all ears at this point.

"Ah, I told him he might want to check out something down at the old Hargrave place. And I'll bet sure as hell, he went down there. Oh shit, I hope he's not in trouble!"

"Show me where he is!" Brick said as he got into his squad car. Ben ran to get into his truck, and the two vehicles tore down the dirt road to a private road not far away.

CHAPTER FOUR

Less than an hour earlier that day, Billy Roy watched as Ben's old pickup truck disappeared down the highway. He turned and got into his patrol car. He thought, "I guess I'll check it out, but first I'll let Juanita know where I'm going." He called the office and told Juanita to call him back in 30 minutes if he didn't check in. Then, he drove down the private road that led back into the boondocks.

It was a twisting little road and went down into a valley, then cut along the side of the valley. He could see a building up ahead. It looked like there was some activity around it. There were four late model cars parked outside and one large truck. Billy Roy eased the squad car up within 100 yards of the building and stopped. "I wonder if I oughta check this out. It doesn't look like anything's wrong. I can hear some activity in there. Maybe I'll just drive on up and see what's going on.

He put the car into gear and drove up and parked behind one of the newer models. He checked his .38 police special that Brick had issued to him, then reached into the glove box and grabbed a small derringer that he shoved into his boot. Billy Roy had always carried a small handgun with him, and he felt that the second gun might come in handy some day. He wasn't expecting trouble, but he'd been taught to look out for it because trouble could show up at any time. He thought it was better to be cautious. He checked his watch. It had only been ten minutes since he had talked to Juanita, so he wasn't going to call her. He had nothing to report anyway.

Billy Roy opened the door, slid out and started walking to the building. He had just walked past the big truck when he felt movement behind him. Before he could turn, something hit him hard on the back of the head, and he passed out.

When Billy Roy came to, he was sitting with his hands tied behind him inside the building. Two scruffy looking men were standing over him. One said, "Golly, I sure did wop the shit out of him. I didn't mean to almost kill him, but I guess I did, didn't I, Dad?"

"Well, son, you damn near killed him, but you *didn't*, and that's not a good thing." The older man turned to Billy Roy. "Deputy, what are you doing out here?"

Billy Roy could hardly get his senses together. His head was throbbing and he could feel a little wetness back there that must have been blood.

"What the hell's going on here?" He said as he tried to gain some control.

"Well son, you just shouldn't go snooping around here without knowing what you're doing, ya know?"

"I didn't know that I was snooping around. I just came to see what you were doing." Billy Roy tried to make it seem like his purpose for being there was just routine.

"Yeah, well you stepped right into a goddamn hornet's nest didn't ya? You sure did screw things up."

Billy Roy looked around and took in the mass of car parts, tires, and wheels scattered all around the building. "Ah, I believe I walked into a chop shop, didn't I?"

The old man folded his arms across his chest. "Well, you might have done that son, and I'm sorry you did. Now what in the hell are we gonna do with ya?"

"Well, the best thing you can do is untie me, and let me take you in. It won't be serious. You got caught with stolen cars in a chop shop…you might get out fairly light. But if you do anything to me you know that's a murder wrap."

"Well, hell I'm sorry that he hurt you. I told him to kill ya!" The two thieves laughed at the old man's statement.

Billy Roy realized that he was in deeper trouble than he originally thought. He needed to keep his cool. He needed to get free from the chair, and yet he couldn't afford to make them mad with him tied up like this. He decided to take a friendly-type approach, while he tried to get his hands free. "That's real nice, fella. By the way who are you?"

"It doesn't make a goddamn who I am!" he snarled at Billy Roy.

"You tell him Dad." Junior was obviously having fun with all of this.

The old man growled, "Yeah, shut up son!"

"What are we gonna do, Dad?"

"Well, ya almost killed him. I guess we'd just better finish it up. 'Cause we sure as hell can't let him get away. Son, you sure do fuck things up!" He scowled at his son.

"I didn't do it, Dad!"

"Ah, yes you did. He probably followed you down here with that last hot car. I told you we had enough to take care of, and that we didn't have to get into full scale business. We're doing fine, just like we were."

"Yeah, but this is a nice one. It'll bring us a bunch."

"Just shut up and let me think." The older Hargrave walked to the door and spit a long stream of tobacco juice. "Damn kid," he mumbled. "What are we gonna do?"

A third man appeared in the room. "I'll tell you what, let's just close this place up and get the hell outa here. Somebody will find him."

"Well, now ain't that smart. We're just gonna run away. Where the hell are we gonna run to?"

"Myself, I got kin in Alabama, and I'm going back there."

"Yeah, you running coward, you. Goddamn, I never should have hired you on. You're just a yellow jacket."

"I ain't either."

"Let me think. Tell you what... let's get him out of here. Son, you take him down by the river there, and why don't you take the shovel with ya, and kinda dispose of him down there, would you do that?"

The younger Hargrave seemed excited by his father's order. "Oh yeah, Pa...I'll take him on down...ah, what do you want me to do with him?

"Well, why don't you take him down and have a little tea party with him," he said sarcastically. "Goddamn, son," he slammed his fist into the wall. Do I have to tell you everything?"

Not wanting to be the target of his father's wrath, the son replied, "Alright, Dad, I'm going."

"Get up here, Deputy!"

Billy Roy looked down and saw his pistol was missing from his holster, but he could feel the derringer down in his boot. "Ok if I can just get my damn hands loose," he thought to himself. Billy Roy was pulled to his feet and pushed out of the building, toward one of the cars parked in the front. The son, whose name was Leonard, got a shovel out of the building, threw it in the back and pushed Billy Roy in the front seat on the passenger side. Leonard ran around the car, got in, backed out and drove down behind the building where the river ran.

It was about a quarter mile drive to the river. Billy Roy didn't see anyone along the way, but was hoping that somebody would show up someplace. He thought, "One good thing is they didn't take my cell phone. How can I get to it?" It was still in his front shirt pocket.

They got down to the river bank, and Leonard said, "Alright, now you stay in here. I gotta get some work done. Damn, you sure did mess things up!" Leonard got out of the car, reached in the backseat and grabbed the shovel. He headed along the bank of the river, found a soft spot and started digging. Even though his hands were still tied behind his back, Billy Roy worked his way out of the car, and stood nearby determining what should be his next move. He knew it would be difficult to run with his hands behind him, and he didn't know if Leonard had a weapon on him, so he decided to take it easy with Leonard and try to get on his good side. He said, "Leonard that sure looks like a lotta hard work."

Leonard turned quickly to see Billy Roy standing there. "Yeah, it is."

"Well, if you'll tie my hands in front, I can help you."

Billy Roy had a nice, friendly smile on his face, so that Leonard wouldn't think he had any ulterior motives. Billy could only hope Leonard was that stupid.

Apparently, Billy Roy was right, because Leonard came over to him, untied his hands, brought Billy Roy's arms to the front and was beginning to retie his hands, when Billy Roy attacked him, taking him to the ground to gain control of him. "Give it up, Leonard," he shouted, but Leonard continued to punch and hit Billy Roy. They started rolling down the short hill toward the water's edge which broke their hold on each other. Both men were quickly getting up, which allowed enough time for Billy Roy to take the derringer out of his boot. When Leonard turned around to face his opponent, he saw the weapon in Billy Roy's hand. This infuriated him, and he quickly charged at Billy Roy, hoping to knock him down and take the gun from him. Unfortunately, the gun went off during the altercation, and Leonard rolled over dead from a shot in the heart. Billy Roy noticed that Leonard had put Billy's revolver inside his belt in the back. "I guess he forgot he had it," Billy Roy said.

CHAPTER FIVE

Billy Roy was stunned. He had never killed a man before. "Damn," he said. Then, quickly he realized that the sound of the gun would bring Leonard's father and the other guy down to the river. He needed help and right away! He reached in his pocket to see if the phone was still there. It was. "Oh, thank God!" He said as he dialed Brick's number.

Brick's phone began ringing. When he saw that it was Billy Roy calling, he quickly answered it. He could hear heavy breathing on the other end, "Billy Roy, are you ok?"

Billy Roy said, "Where are you located, Sheriff?"

"Well, Ben and I are on our way to the building he sent you to earlier. Are you there?"

"Yes, but I'm down behind the building near the river." Without taking a breath, Billy Roy started quickly telling Brick everything that happened. "Sheriff, they were going to kill me. One of the dudes, and I were fighting, and I had a chance to pull out my derringer, and then he charged at me again, and the gun went off, and he's dead."

"Oh God! Slow down, Billy Roy, and take a deep breath."

"The other two guys will be looking for me, I'm sure they heard the shot."

"Ok, we're at the property now. Well I'm about maybe 150 yards from the building."

"Ok, Sheriff, why don't you leave the patrol car there and come up on foot. I'm gonna walk back up there...I'm down by the river, down behind the building. I think between the three of us we can jump 'em and probably settle this."

"Ah, ok. You got your gun?"

"Yah, yah, I just took it back from the boy here."

"Alright, I'll move up and we'll go in when you get here." Brick motioned to Ben as he walked to his car.

"Ok!"

"Be careful!" Brick told Ben what had happened and encouraged him to stay in his car.

"No, way!" Ben was determined. "I got him into this mess, and I wanna help him out of it."

The sheriff checked his weapons. He had a .357, as well as, his .38 police special. He often carried both pistols, just in case. He got out of the car. "Here," he said as he gave the .38 to Ben. "Be careful. And let me do all the talking."

"Yes, Sir."

They started making their way toward the building trying to keep a low profile. They were just about to the building, when they saw Billy Roy. Using hands signals, they communicated their plan. They both came in towards the big door and burst into the garage just as old man Hargrave and the other man were on their way out to look for Leonard.

"Drop your guns and put your hands up. You're under arrest."

They both froze. "What do you mean we're under arrest?."

"You heard me! You gotta chop shop going here, as well as, attempted murder."

"What do you mean attempted murder? We didn't do nothing."

Old man Hargrave realized that Billy Roy was standing there with his gun drawn, too. "Where's my boy?" He asked.

Billy Roy spoke up. "Your boy is dead."

Hargrave was shocked. "What!" He gasped, "You killed my boy?"

"That's right. He tried to kill me, just as you told him to."

"Wait a minute, I didn't tell him to do nothing."

"Yeah you did, and I'm going to swear to it in court. You're both going to jail for a long time." Billy Roy was determined.

"Hey, hey, I didn't have anything to do with it," said the other man. "I'm just here working for Mr. Hargrave, and I'll testify...to whatever you say."

"Oh, you will?" Brick was curious to see where this would go.

"Yes," said the man nervously. "Cause I ain't got nothing to do with this. I didn't mind stealing cars, but they ain't getting me for no murder wrap."

Brick couldn't believe the guy just admitted to car theft. "What a dummy," he thought. "OK, both of you put your hands behind you."

Brick and Billy Roy put handcuffs on them and lead them out to the cars.

"I had no idea this business was here." Brick said as they put the men in the cars.

"I never would have found it if it hadn't been for Ben telling me." Billy Roy was looking at Ben. They both thanked Ben for his help.

"I'm just glad you're ok, Billy Roy." Ben said as he shook Billy's hand.

"Sheriff...what about the body of the dead man?"

"We'll call the coroner's office out for that, and because it's an officer-involved shooting, the state troopers will have to investigate it. Let's call them out here, then get George to transport the old man back to the jail for booking. I'll take the younger one back in my car, while you secure the shooting scene until the coroner has completed his investigation and removed

Leonard's body. That way, you'll also be here in case the troopers need to ask you any questions."

"Yes, sir," replied Billy Roy.

Brick and George put the prisoners in their vehicles and drove to the office.

Juanita and Bonnie looked up as Brick and George escorted the two men into the office. "Sheriff, what do you need me to do?" Bonnie asked, as she quickly stood up.

Juanita chimed in at the same time, but along a different track. "I tried to get Billy Roy, Sheriff, but...."

Brick was obviously not in a position to deal with that at the moment. "Never mind Juanita, we'll take care of that in a minute," he said as he turned to Bonnie. "Bonnie, can you help George?"

"Yes, Sir," she said as she assisted George with the older Hargrave.

Juanita was on a roll. "OK...Sheriff what are you going to do with those two men?"

"We're gonna put them in cells." His patience was running thin at this point.

"Oh...OK," she responded.

"Juanita, where are the keys to the jail cell?"

"Ah, which key is that, Sheriff?"

"Remember I gave you the big ring that had four keys on it?"

"Yeah, I remember now...hmmm...I know I put them some place." She looked up as if she was trying to get a vision in her head about where she left them.

"Juanita, come on, come on!"

Just then Bonnie left the prisoner with George, ran up to the desk, moved some things on the desk, picked up the keys and handed them to Brick. Brick was very relieved that at least one of the clerks was on top of it.

"Oh yeah, I put them right under my lunch sack."

Brick and George took the prisoners into the cell block. They booked the two prisoners in, and took their handcuffs off. They let each man make a phone call, then put the old man into a cell at the opposite end of the jail area so that he could not communicate with any other prisoners.

On the way into town, Tom, after being advised of his rights, had told Brick all about the shop's operation and each person's part in it. He agreed to testify in court. Brick took Tom into an interrogation room, read him his rights again, and had him write down in his own words everything that he had told Brick in the car, including the old man's instructions to Leonard to kill Billy Roy. Brick had Bonnie witness Tom's signing of his statement and he also recorded Tom's confession on a tape recorder for later use in court.

By the time all this was done the state troopers had finished with Billy Roy at the scene of the shooting and released him to return to the sheriff's office. He was in the process of telling them about his ordeal when Bonnie noticed Billy Roy was starting to stagger a bit, and went over to check on him. "Are you ok?" she asked him.

Brick answered, "He's had a day of it. I need to get him to a doctor."

"Ah ya, I'm feeling a little bit funny," he said, as he put his hands on his head.

"Well, let's do it right now!"

Brick helped him into the car, and they headed out to the doctor's office.

As Bonnie shut the door to the building, Juanita said, "We got us some business now. Hot dog!" Bonnie just rolled her eyes and returned to her desk.

After Brick learned that the doctor was going to keep Billy Roy in the hospital overnight for observation, he returned to the location of the chop shop where the Department of Public Safety crime scene techs were taking inventory of all the stolen parts found in the Hargraves' shop. The detectives investigating the shooting had already left the crime scene so Brick verified that the DPS techs would finish their part of the investigation, and then he returned to his office.

He later learned that two of the cars had been stolen in New Mexico, thus making it a federal case. He also learned that two state troopers would come in the morning to pick up the two prisoners and escort them to San Antonio to be turned over to federal authorities.

Brick was pleased with how Billy Roy handled the situation, even though he did get hurt. "At least he's gonna be ok," Brick said to himself.

CHAPTER SIX

Friday morning Brick arrived at the office at eight o'clock to find Juanita already working diligently at her desk, and his deputies were out on patrol. It had been a long evening, first making sure that Billy Roy was recovering from his injuries, and then finishing the statements from Billy Roy at the hospital, and from Tom who was locked up back in the county jail. It was obvious that the state troopers and the FBI were going to be doing the lion's share of the work of preparing the cases for their respective prosecuting attorneys. Brick did not want to have the prisoners removed from his control until his department's actions were completely documented and probable cause for the initial investigation of the chop shop and the subsequent killing of Leonard by his deputy was established beyond a doubt.

Brick had heard of several situations in which a city or county law enforcement department had made what they thought was a simple arrest for drugs or theft, only to find out later that the actions of the criminal was part of a much larger picture than they had the resources to properly investigate or prosecute. When getting the state police, the DEA, or the FBI involved, the larger organizations wrote their reports and findings to make their departments look good at the expense of the smaller local police. One instance had even resulted in the local department being sued for false arrest while the FBI was credited with breaking up the entire criminal operation. Brick was not going to allow that to happen in this case, especially since it involved one of his officers having shot and killed a suspect.

Brick asked Juanita if she had made a pot of coffee yet. He had slept as long as he could and did not take the time to eat breakfast. He couldn't wait to get a heavy dose of caffeine into his tired veins. She poured him a cup of the freshly brewed coffee in a big mug.

"Oooo, that's too hot to drink right now," he said, "Please set the mug on my desk."

Brick looked up to see the two state troopers walk into the office. "We've come to pick up the prisoners from yesterday's chop shop arrests. They want us to get them over to San Antonio as quickly as possible."

"Hi, I'm Sheriff Brick Walls," he said as he shook their hands. "I'll get them."

Brick went back to the cell block, unlocked Tom's door and brought him to the front office. He explained to the two troopers that Tom had cooperated fully with him and given him statements both about the operations of the chop shop and about old man Hargrave telling his son Leonard to take Deputy Bryant out back and kill him. Brick did not want Hargrave riding close to Tom where he could hurt him or scare him into changing his story. The troopers explained that they were in separate vehicles, so that had no chance of happening, and that they would keep a close eye on Hargrave in San Antonio to make sure he did not get around Tom for any reason. Brick then went back into the cell block to get Hargrave.

"Put your hands behind your backs," the troopers ordered.

Tom did what he was told, but the older man, Hargrave said, "No you're not gonna take me!" He quickly pushed the two troopers knocking them back against the wall. Hargrave started reaching for one of their guns. His back was to Juanita who instantly picked up the cup of hot coffee, and slammed it hard against Hargrave's skull which in turn caused the coffee to spill all over his head.

"Oh, Lord," he screamed as he sank to his knees. The two troopers quickly handcuffed him and dried off his head. He wasn't burnt but he could feel the stinging sensation for a while.

"That's a brave little lady you've got there, Sheriff," the trooper said as he finished putting the handcuffs on Tom and moved both of the men out of the door to the awaiting squad cars.

"Yup, surprises come in small packages, don't they?" Brick waved as the cars pulled out onto the highway.

As he walked back into the office, he said, "I'll tell you, I never thought you could do that Juanita."

"Well, Sheriff, they tried to mess up my office, and I just got it cleaned up. Now look at it. Now I've got to clean up the floor again." Bonnie went for the mop to help.

"Juanita, you did a good job. That was a brave thing you did."

"Sheriff, I just couldn't let them rough you up or rough up the troopers there, now could I? I did good, didn't I?" She said with a big smile on her face.

"You did real good!" Brick said walking back into his office with a smile on his face and shaking his head.

That afternoon the newspaper carried the story and had a picture of Juanita holding the coffee cup. It was the talk of the town for a few days.

Meanwhile, in an office in Mexico City, Carlos Vega was seated at a table with four of his top henchmen. The atmosphere was heavy with Carlos's anger. "Damn it! I'm tired of waiting for us to find out who in hell disrupted our business in Texas. Whoever it was will pay greatly for the loss of the airplane, the drugs, and the one million dollars. I've spent some time and money looking into this, and someone told me there's a man named Brick Walls involved with this and actually took the money. I want it back, and I want it back now! Do any of you know anything about this bastard?" No one acknowledged having any information about Brick other than what they had been told by remaining dealers in the pipeline in Texas. Of course, Carlos already had that information.

Carlos turned to his right, "Roberto, I need you to go to Texas tomorrow and find out what you can about this Walls guy and see if we have a chance of getting our money and drugs back. We need to get re-established now!"

"Si, Carlos, I will leave tomorrow. I'll find this asshole."

"Bueno!" Carlos knew if anyone could come up with the information, it would be Roberto. He had worked for Carlos for many years and knew the business inside and out. He knew how to solve problems…whether by negotiation or by force. Roberto preferred force, but could negotiate if he had to.

"The rest of you will get ready to resume our business in the south Texas area. We have much of our product ready to go to the U.S. but we must establish new contacts for this route, and that will be your job. Leave tomorrow for the States and re-establish our routes, pick-ups and deliveries. Call me daily and let me know your progress. Now, leave!" The four men wasted no time exiting the room. Carlos sat back in his chair with an evil smile on his face. "You just think you got away, Senor Walls." He picked up his cigar and took a long puff, blowing the smoke slowly into the air.

CHAPTER SEVEN

It was almost time for Juanita's shift to end. As she was putting up the documents she would send to the court the next day, the phone rang. "Sheriff's office...This is Juanita. How may I help you?"

A male's voice on the other end sounded distraught as he started telling Juanita about the shouting and screaming he was hearing coming from a couple of houses down from him. "Is there any way we can get a deputy over here to investigate this?"

"Of course, Sir, but I need to get some information from you first. Now, what is your name and address?"

"My name is Patrick Simmons and I live at 303 Garden Lane. Now can you send someone?" It was evident he didn't want to spend any more time on the phone with Juanita.

"I understand, Mr. Simmons, but in order for us to do our job properly, we'll need just a little more information. Do you know the address of the house where the screaming is coming from?"

"No. Hey listen, are you sending someone or not?"

"One last question. How long has this screaming been going on and can you still hear it?"

"Lady, this screaming has been going on for about fifteen minutes. Now, I'm going to hang up and see if I can hear it again. Good bye."

Juanita immediately called George who was the deputy on duty that evening. "Hey, Juanita, what's going on?"

"George, there has been a report of screaming coming from a house in the 300 block of Garden Lane. Apparently it's been going on for about fifteen minutes. Mr. Simmons reported this disturbance. He lives at 303 Garden Lane."

"Ok, Juanita. I'm headed that way." George hung up the phone and picked up the speed in the squad car. It took him about eight minutes to get to the neighborhood. As he approached the 300 block, he rolled his window down to listen for any sign of a disturbance.

Almost immediately George could hear shouting coming from the middle of the block and he pulled to a stop in front of 307 Garden Lane. Just as he was getting out of his squad car, Juanita called again to say that a female complainant living at 307 Garden Lane had called to report being beaten by her drunken husband. George told her that he was at the location and then headed up to the house. Juanita told him that Deputy Albert Watkins was at the office and about to come on duty so she would send him to Garden Lane to back him up on the call.

George knocked on the front door then stepped back to the side of it, as he had been trained to do, in case one of the residents fired a shot through the door. The front door opened and he was met by a middle-aged bleached blond woman who already had a swollen eye and blood on her face from a cut on her lip.

"Come in Sheriff, and take this wife-beating son of a bitch to jail before he kills me!" she shouted as a man that George presumed to be her husband came up behind her.

"Well, well, you sure are Johnny-On-The-Spot, aren't you Mr. Officer? The bitch just now called and you're already at the front door. That's some kind of service for a County Mounty, isn't it? You people usually take a good thirty minutes to get over here when she's called you before."

George could smell the strong smell of whiskey coming off the man as he entered the house. The man inside was about five feet, ten inches tall and weighed almost two-hundred pounds. He appeared to be about forty years old. The woman stepped out of the way, so George could come on into the house and face the belligerent husband.

"Now everybody just calm down and let's see if we can get this worked out peaceably." George told them. He was trying to stall for time to give Albert a chance to get there in case this drunk wanted to fight. "Ma'am, I see that your face is bruised – are you ok?"

"Hell, NO! I'm not OK! Just look what he did to me. I won't be able to go out in public for a week or more without having to be made up like a twenty-dollar whore."

"I meant, do you require medical attention? Do you need me to call an ambulance for you so that you can get checked out at the hospital?"

"No, I don't need no damn ambulance. But I'm not staying here with him (pointing to her husband) while he's this way. Can't you just put him in jail until he sobers up and then let him come on back to the house?"

"I'm afraid it doesn't work that way Mrs...."

"Sampson, Elaine Sampson, and my husband's name is Jack Sampson."

About that time Albert arrived at the house and came to the door. It was still open but he knocked anyway.

"Come on in, Officer," said the husband. "Pretty soon we'll have enough people here for a damn party. So which one of you two is going to be the hero and whip my ass?"

"There's no need for any of that, Mr. Sampson. Why don't you come out in the front yard with me and give your wife a chance to cool off for a bit? That way you can tell me your version of what happened while she is telling Deputy Watkins her side of this argument."

"Aw, hell. Alright. I usually don't even get a chance to say anything...they just haul my ass off to jail as soon as she starts bitching at them. Just let me get my drink."

"Why don't you leave the drink inside for a few minutes and let's just talk this over and see what started the argument," George told him. They both walked out the front door.

Sampson immediately began to tell him the details about the fight that he had had with his wife, and as he was doing so, George slowly walked him down the sidewalk toward the street. In Texas, it is legal to be intoxicated on your own property, but if he could get Sampson to step into the street with him, he could take him to jail for being drunk in public. Then, he wouldn't have to get the wife to come to the station to give a statement for a case that she would just have dismissed as soon as he sobered up.

As they got to the end of the sidewalk, George stepped into the street, but Sampson stopped short and would not step off his property. He had obviously been down this road before. As Sampson swayed back and forth right at the edge of the street, George had a fleeting thought that Sampson might just go ahead and fall into the street, but that did not happen. George would have to try and reason with him in hopes of getting Sampson (or his wife) to stay somewhere else for the night so that peace could be restored.

"You know, Mr. Sampson, all of this will probably blow over in the morning and the two of you will kiss and make up and everything will be ok. Have your arguments ever ended up in blows before?"

Just in case the wife did intend to file charges and stick with them, George wanted to get an admission from the husband that he had struck her in anger during the argument.

"Naw, usually there's just a bunch of shouting and yelling, but tonight she really, really pissed me off, and I belted her a couple of times to shut her damned mouth up. I didn't mean to hurt her none, but I guess I'm a little drunker than I thought I was."

"Do you have a place you can go to tonight to give things a chance to cool off for a while, or does she have any relatives she can spend the night with?" George asked.

"Yeah, she has a sister who lives in town that she can stay with, if it comes to that. I'm sorry now that I hit her, and I really don't want to go to jail. Can you help me out here, Deputy?" Sampson seemed to have settled down somewhat, now that impending jail time was looming in his very near future. But George knew that to leave them together tonight would probably result in another fight because she called the officers out there in the first place.

"Let's go back inside and see what she thinks about staying with her sister for the night. I have to warn you, Mr. Sampson, that if she decides to press charges, I will have to take you under arrest. Also, it's only a Class C misdemeanor for an assault, but if you decide you want to fight me and the other deputy, you're going to be looking at some serious jail time after you get out of the hospital," George told him.

"I don't need to go to no hospital...she didn't hit me this time," Sampson stated.

"I know, but if you decide you want to fight me and Deputy Watkins, you *will* be going to the hospital before you go to jail. I just thought I'd warn you up front."

The two men went back inside to find that Mrs. Sampson had calmed down quite a bit and did not want to file assault charges against her husband, thereby putting her only source of income in jail. She agreed to take the car and go to her sister's to sleep for the night, and the husband agreed to go to bed and sleep it off. George got Albert to follow Mrs. Sampson to her sister's house in town, while George parked down the street for a short time to make sure that Mr. Sampson didn't decide to leave the house instead of passing out. After about fifteen minutes, it was evident that Sampson was not leaving. The lights were off and there was no sign of activity, so George drove to the office to get his reports finished and turned in, then headed for his house. His shift was over for the night.

CHAPTER EIGHT

It was a beautiful, sunny Saturday morning. Red jumped up on the side of the bed to wake up Brick. "Good morning, Big Fella," Brick said as he petted the soft, auburn fur on Red's head. "I guess you're telling me you want to go out, right?" He sat up as Red barked happily. "I'll take that as a yes," he said as he put on his jeans and went to open the back door. Red bolted past him and into the back yard, looking back to make sure that Brick was following him.

Brick took a deep breath of the fresh air then ran with the dog in the yard. Red loved to run, especially when Brick was part of his game of chase. It tired them both out, but it became a daily routine that they both enjoyed tremendously. When Red finally decided to drink some water, Brick went for the hose and watered Mom's Garden. The herbs were growing quickly, and several of them gave out a delightful smell. It made Brick remember the foods that his mother cooked using those very same herbs from her garden. She was a wonderful cook, and he missed the meals she made. Although Sally was an excellent cook herself, nothing could come close to the memories he cherished of growing up eating the delicacies his mother prepared. He missed those days…and he missed her. He smiled as he shut down the water and went into the house to feed Red and fix himself some coffee and breakfast.

It was about six o'clock that evening when Brick started to get ready for his birthday date with Sally. After his shower, he shaved again and then put on a pair of dark gray slacks and a short sleeved multi-colored checked shirt. Brick was still in pretty good shape and probably looked five or six years younger than his actual age. He wanted to look nice for Sally and professional for his co-workers. He studied himself in the mirror. "Not too bad," he said to himself smiling. As he walked to the front door, Red ran to him and rubbed up against his clean slacks. "Swell," he said as he grabbed some tape from the desk drawer and tried to get the dog hair off his leg. "Alright, Red, I'll be gone for a while. You guard the house." He locked the house, got in his truck, and drove off to pick up Sally.

He parked out in front, walked up to the door and rang the bell. The door flew open.

"Happy Birthday, Brick!" Sally said as she wrapped her arms around his neck, giving him a big hug and kiss. Brick was taken aback, but happy. It felt good to have Sally in his arms. He wanted to just stand there and continue to hold her and kiss her, but he knew that he was still hurting from the loss of Helen, and he wasn't ready to commit to a long-term relationship.

Brick looked in Sally's eyes. Her eyes were deep blue and still as beautiful as they were when they dated in high school. The message in her eyes was very clear to Brick, and it would have been so easy to let them take him in. However, he realized he needed to back off for the moment for fear of saying or doing something that he might regret later. Besides, they needed to get out to Bob's place where the birthday party was being held. It wouldn't do for the guest of honor to be late for his own party.

"Thank you, Sally," he said as he took her hand and led her to the truck. She looked very cute in her beautiful short sleeved white dress with ruffles on the skirt. "She hasn't changed much since high school," he mused to himself, smiling as he walked her to the vehicle.

Bob had invited all of the staff from the Sheriff's office and their wives or dates, as well as, two mutual friends and their wives. "Happy Birthday!" They all shouted as Brick and Sally entered the room. Champagne was served, and they all lifted their glasses to toast the guest of honor, "To Brick, a great man and a great sheriff!" "To Brick!" They all replied and clicked their glasses together.

Brick was smiling at Sally, and as they looked into each other's eyes, they raised their glasses, and took a sip. "Maybe I'm being too cautious," he thought to himself, and took another sip.

Bob brought out a barbeque pork loin that he had fixed earlier that afternoon. They all sat down to a delicious smoked pork dinner with Irish potatoes and carrots. Earlier that day, Sally had dropped off a delightful cheese cake from the restaurant that she made herself. It only had a few candles on it. Sally explained as she brought the cake to the table, "I couldn't get all 47 candles on this cake. It violated the fire code restrictions for the café." Everyone had a good laugh at Brick's expense on that one, and Sally hoped that it didn't make Brick angry or embarrassed.

Brick said, "I couldn't have blown them all out anyway!" They all laughed again. Actually, Sally had arranged the few candles to say "47". They all sang happy birthday, then Brick bent over the cake and said, "1-2-3." He blew hard at the flames. The candles in the 4 went out but not all of the candles in the 7…two candles were still burning. He blew again and this time he got them all. Everyone applauded and laughed. Brick said, "See, I'm not as full of hot air as you said I was." They all laughed again and continued to have a good evening, playing card games, singing songs, and telling stories of times they all remembered of Brick…going back to the days when Brick was the football hero.

Bob spoke of the story of how Brick got his name. He told the others that during one game, the announcer made the comment, "When players run into that Walls boy, it's like running into a brick wall." And he was known as Brick Walls ever since. Brick thought, "I'm never gonna live that one down."

The party broke up about eleven-thirty. It had been a long week at work, and some of the staff had to work on Sunday. Brick and Sally said their goodbyes and got into the truck. It was quiet, as he drove her home.

When they arrived, he went to open the door for Sally. "I really enjoyed this, Sally. Maybe we can get together again sometime soon."

Sally didn't want Brick to leave yet. "Would you like to come in for a drink? Or just come in to talk?" Her invitation was very alluring, and Brick wasn't sure what would happen if he said yes.

"Well, I can walk you to the door at least," he said as Sally took his hand and smiled at him.

When they arrived at the front door, Sally tried one more time to get Brick to agree to come in the house. "Won't you please come in?"

As much as he wanted to stay, he said, "Sally, I really hope we can get together again soon. Having you with me tonight made my birthday very special. Thank you so much." He looked into her eyes again, then gave her a long good night kiss, and headed back to the truck.

"I'll call you tomorrow." Brick said as Sally waved to him from the front porch. Both had the feeling that this relationship had just become a little deeper.

CHAPTER NINE

The early morning sun shone through the window waking Brick from a deep sleep. He rolled over and looked at the clock. "Six thirty...time to get moving," he said as he sat up and looked at Red who was stretching on the floor. "It's Monday morning and time to get up, Red." The big dog stood up, shook himself then excitedly walked to the door. It was obvious he was ready for the new day. Brick quickly put his clothes on and went to let Red out of the back door. "Hurry up, Boy. Today we're gonna take a walk before we go into work."

While Red was outside, Brick fixed himself a cup of coffee and filled up the dog's dish. When he let Red back inside, he noticed the thermometer on his porch was already at 85 degrees. "Looks like it's going to be another hot day in South Texas," he said as he took his last sip of coffee. "Come on, Red. Let's get in the truck." Red followed Brick outside and jumped in the front seat. "Good, Boy!" Brick said as he shut the door, got in, and started the engine.

They drove out to the acreage his father had left him. There was a small pond on the east side of the property. When Brick opened the truck door, Red immediately took off running toward the water. He liked to get in and splash around. Brick hollered, "Whoa, Red, no. Not today." The Irish setter stopped at the command and turned around to see Brick motioning him to come back. "Come on, Red, let's take a quick walk." Red looked back at the water, walked over to get a drink then ran back to Brick. "Good Boy, Red! Good Boy!" Brick said as he petted the dog's head and started walking to the west side of the land.

It hadn't rained in over three weeks, so the field was dry and dusty. There were lots of grasshoppers and cicadas along with dragon flies and various other bugs making their way through the field. Sometimes Red would chase the ones that got too close to his face. After about twenty minutes, Brick decided it was time to get to work. "Come on, Boy, let's go!" They both got into the truck, and Brick made his way back to the house to get ready for the day.

Back at the house, Brick put on his short sleeved uniform shirt and a light weight pair of khaki pants along with his boots. He went to check on Red and made sure he had fresh water for the day. "Ok, Boy, I'll be back later," he said as he locked the door and went to his squad car.

On his way to the office, he stopped by the doughnut shop for two regular doughnuts and a cup of black coffee.

"I wonder what today is gonna bring," he said as he took a sip of coffee and turned up the radio to hear his favorite country music.

As he pulled into the parking lot he noticed that both of his clerks were already there. He was pleased that things seemed to be working out with the clerks and the deputies he hired. Even though a couple of them were a little slow at their jobs, they were enthusiastic, hard workers. Brick smiled as he entered the office.

Bonnie was on the phone when he walked in. She looked up and smiled, "Sheriff, it's for you."

"I'll take it in my office, Bonnie."

"Yes, sir."

Brick put down his coffee and answered the phone. "This is Sheriff Walls, how can I help you?"

"Hi, Brick, this is Bob. Have you had your breakfast yet?"

"Hi, Bob. Yes, I have. What's up?"

"Are you busy right now, 'cause I've got something to tell you." Brick noticed that Bob didn't sound like himself. He could tell something wasn't quite right.

"No, I'm not busy, Bob. Come on over."

"Ok, I'll be there in about ten minutes." Bob hung up the phone.

Brick looked over some papers on his desk, wondering what Bob had to tell him. Juanita came in with a cheerful smile on her face, "Good morning, Sheriff. How are you?"

Brick smiled, "Good morning, Juanita. I'm doing fine."

"Is there anything special I need to do besides just the normal stuff?"

"No, nothing has come up yet this morning."

"Ok, well I'll just start going over the reports from the weekend happenings." She left his office and went to her desk.

Brick shook his head and went back to looking over the papers on his desk, when Bob entered the front office and asked to see the sheriff. Brick stood up, "Hi, Bob. Come on in."

Bob shook Brick's hand as Brick shut the office door.

"Hey, thanks again for the birthday party Saturday. Sally and I really had a great time."

"You're quite welcome, Brick. I think everyone enjoyed themselves. It's good to take some time off from the regular routine and have some fun with friends."

"Yes, it is. Now tell me what's going on?"

Bob seemed a little uncomfortable. "I'd like to tell you what happened last night." Brick nodded his head to continue. "You know down behind the pool hall and bar there's a large building where we play poker on Sunday evenings. It's just a friendly game." Bob didn't want Brick to think they were doing anything illegal.

"Yeah, yeah, I know about it," Brick said. "It's ok as long as you don't get rowdy and tear things up." He smiled.

"Well, last night we started a game. Jake was there, you know he runs the bar, also Henry Pearson, his bartender was there. There was Fred Anders, you know he's the local real estate guy."

"Yeah, I know him." Brick was thinking that he was going to regret hearing the rest of this story.

"And Ned Hanson...you know Ned. He runs the gas station down the street."

"Yeah, I know Ned."

"And of course, I was playing. There was also another guy there, I think his name was Jack Jones. He's a plumber. He's kinda new here."

"No, I don't think I've ever met him."

"Well, anyway...we all had a beer or two, and the game was going along real good when it seems that Ned thought something was funny the way that Jack Jones was dealing. He thought maybe he had stacked the deck or something. So Ned watched as Jack dealt. He knew the bottom card was the five of spades. As the hand progressed, it appeared that Jack had need of a five of spades. He had the four, six and seven showing. We were playing seven card stud. Just as Jack was dealing the last cards, Ned said 'Tell you what, if the five of spades shows up, I'm gonna whoop your ass.'

And Jack said, 'What do you mean?' Ned told him, 'I know that card is on the bottom of the stack and it better still be there!' Jack threw the deck of cards on the table and said 'By God, I'm not going to play anymore.' 'I'm gonna come over there and whoop your ass!'"

"Well, we couldn't have a fight break out and so since it was at Jake's place he said, 'Keep going. Leave. We don't want any fighting.' So anyway Jack left, and we started to deal again. About twenty minutes later the door burst open. It was Jack Jones, and he had a .25 caliber pistol in one hand and a .38 in the other. He went up to Ned and said, 'All right you big mouth son-of-a-bitch, what have you got to say?' Ned looked up at him, sweat pouring from his brow said, 'I'm a big mouth son-of-a-bitch.' Jack started walking toward Ned, saying 'I'm gonna kick your ass now.'"

"Two of the boys got up and one of them said, 'No, no violence here. I want you to leave. Leave now! We don't want no fights and no shooting.' Jack said, 'I'll leave, but I'll be waiting outside.' Well, he left, and after a lot of discussion about it, the game was started up again, but without a lot of enthusiasm. Fred said, 'I think we ought to break it up and go home. We leave at midnight anyway, and it's already eleven o'clock.'"

"Ned said, 'Do you think he's waiting outside?' 'Well it's possible,' said Jake, 'but let's play some more. We don't have to leave right now. It's not midnight yet.' The rest of the guys shook their heads in agreement, and we started up the game again."

"Midnight came around, and Fred said, "It's midnight, and I'm leaving. If I see him out there, I'll come back in and tell ya.'

Ned said, 'Wait a minute, let's play some more, we ought to play a little longer.' Everybody else wanted to leave, too. Henry said, 'No it's time to go home. We've all got to work tomorrow. I don't think he'd be out there waiting for you, but we'll look around and see.'

"As they left the building they looked around for Jack, but didn't see him anywhere. Henry stuck his head back in the door, 'It's ok Ned. He's not here. It's ok to go home.' Ned said, 'Well, wait just a minute until I get in my car, would ya?' The guys agreed to wait until he was in his car. As he started to drive off, he shouted, 'I'll see you boys tomorrow, I hope.' Well, the boys kinda laughed about what had happened. They didn't really think it would have gotten to the shooting stage anyway. But it sure was hairy for a while."

Brick nodded his head in agreement. "Was he cheating?"

Bob shook his head saying, "Naw, after Jack left the poker game, one of the players picked up the deck he had thrown on the table and the five of spades was still on the bottom of the deck. Henry called me a few minutes ago to tell me that Ned met with

Jack this morning at the café and apologized to him. Apparently they decided to shake hands and drop it."

Brick was mulling the story over in his mind. He looked at Bob and said, "It looks like they were able to make amends. I'm not going to look at this as a threat to anybody. We'll just leave it at that."

"I appreciate that, Brick. I don't think anybody is going to complain. I just wanted you to know."

"Well, thanks a lot. I won't say anything."

Bob started to get up, "Ok, well I'm gonna go over to see how the animals are doing. I'll talk to you later." They shook hands, and he left.

Brick sighed a sigh of relief and smiled as he thought to himself, "I love Mondays!!"

That evening Brick decided to take Red out to his property in the country. As usual, Brick left Red in the truck while he went to go unlock the gate. He was in the process of opening the gate when something caught his eye. It was a medium sized rattlesnake laying there at the gate, right next to Brick's foot. "Ah shit!" Brick said and without thinking, he quickly reached down and grabbed the snake at the back of his head with his left hand before the snake could bite him. The snake immediately wrapped itself tightly around Brick's wrist and arm. At that moment Brick realized he couldn't release it without getting bit. He was going to have to get some help.

Brick walked back to the truck and carefully slid onto the seat. Red saw the snake and started barking trying his best to get over to the other side of the seat. "No, no, Red." Brick was trying to hold the snake still with his left hand and push Red away with his right hand. "You stay over there. Sit and hush. You're not going to get this snake. Hell, you'll end up getting us both bitten." It was obvious Red wanted to go after the serpent; however, he did what he was ordered to do and sat down, growling the whole time. "Yeah, that's the same way I feel, buddy, but right now we're just gonna hold it until I can get some help." Brick started the truck and backed out driving one handed, then headed for Dr. Bob's vet clinic.

He pulled into the clinic parking lot, and feeling a little sheepish, he called Bob to meet him outside the door. Then Brick carefully got out of the truck, leaving Red to continue to growl.

Bob opened the clinic door just as Brick got there. He couldn't believe his eyes. "Oh my god! What have you got there?" Bob was focused on the snake which was trying to untangle itself from Brick's arm.

"Well, I thought I'd bring you a little present today. I'm not sure if he's a friend of mine or not. I don't think so though, the way he's hissing and rattling. I thought you might help me find a way to get him off my arm without anyone getting bit."

Bob started to laugh, "You know, you're down right lucky that I have a dog in here trying to give birth to some puppies, or I would have been in bed after being up so late last night at the poker game."

"Yeah, yeah. Just help me get this demon off my arm."

Bob laughed as he opened the door for Brick, "Ok let's see what we can do. Come on."

Brick followed Bob into the patient area, "Are you sure you don't just want to pet him?"

"No, I don't think I want to pet him. Now hold still." Bob picked up a large pair of sharp dog grooming shears and cut off the snake's head without cutting Brick. The rest of the snake's body slowly slithered off Brick's arm and fell to the floor.

As Bob was carefully disposing of the snake body pieces, Brick was rubbing his left arm. "Damn, I sure am glad to have this thing off my arm."

Bob laughed and asked, "Do you realize how lucky you were not to get bitten? How did you get yourself in this position anyway?"

Brick shook his head, "I don't know, but I'm not gonna do that again. I can guarantee you!" They both laughed. "Hey, thanks a lot, Bob. You are a life saver."

Bob shook Brick's hand and gave him a pat on the back, "Hey, what are friends for?"

"See ya later," Brick said as he went back to the truck. Red was anxious to examine Brick's left arm for any signs of the snake. Brick let him sniff and then lick his arm to reassure him that the sidewinder was gone. Red wagged his tail. It was obvious he was happy there was no snake. Red was happy…Brick was happy…so Brick started the truck. "I love Mondays," he said to himself as he headed for home.

CHAPTER TEN

Tuesday afternoon, Juanita was cleaning her desk getting ready to call it a day when Billy Roy came in and poured himself a cup of coffee. He walked over to her desk, sat on the edge of it and said, "I've been thinking about that thing you did when you poured coffee on that prisoner who was trying to escape. I never did tell you how brave you were."

"Well, thank you, Billy Roy," Juanita said, "but you were brave, too. You got hit on the head and passed out and then you had to shoot that guy. You are real brave in my book, you know it?"

"Well, I guess we're a couple of brave people."

"It appears that way," she said with a flirtatious smile.

Billy Roy took a deep breath. "You know...are you brave enough to go out on a date with me...a couple of brave people, ya know?"

"Well, if you're brave enough to meet my mother, 'cause I don't go with anybody unless mama says it's ok."

Billy Roy's eyes got big. "Your mother? Geeze, I've never had to be interviewed by a girl's mother."

Juanita snickered, "Well, you do in this case if you want to go out with me."

"Ah, is she hard to get along with?" He asked showing dread fear on his face.

"Naw, naw...she hasn't killed a boyfriend yet."

"Well, that's nice to know." Billy Roy breathed a sigh of relief. "When would be a good time to come over and meet your mother?" He couldn't believe he was really asking this question... let alone going to follow through with it.

"Well..." she thought for a second, "How about tonight?"

"Ah, well...I'm not working tonight, and you're not either, so I guess tonight it is. Supposing I come over about seven o'clock, and if it's ok with your mother, I'll take you out to a movie. There's a good one showing downtown." He smiled a nervous smile.

Juanita smiled back, "Ok, I'll see ya about seven." She finished putting up her paperwork and left. When she got home she told her mother what had happened.

"Well, is this boy dependable?" She was very adamant about this subject.

"Oh yes. He's a deputy sheriff and works every day. He's brave. He's a good guy...and he's kinda handsome, too!" She giggled as she finished describing Billy Roy.

"Well, I'll look at him. Do you really want to go out with him?" She looked straight into Juanita's eyes for the truth.

"Of course I do, Mom, if it's ok with you."

Juanita's mother sighed, "Alright, I'll check him out." She shook her head and watched as Juanita quickly ran upstairs to get ready for her date.

It was seven o'clock, and Billy Roy took a deep breath as he knocked on the door. He quickly checked his shirt to make sure it was all buttoned up correctly. He was hoping his blue slacks and western-style shirt would meet with Juanita's mother's approval.

He heard someone come to the door. "Well, here we go," he said to himself as he took another deep breath.

To his delight it was Juanita who opened the door to let him in. "Hi, Billy Roy. Oooo don't you look handsome. Come on in."

Billy Roy was glad that his choice of clothes appeared to be fine with Juanita. Now all he had to do was impress her mom and then they could get out of there. He followed Juanita into the living room where a middle-aged woman with a stern looking face was standing. Juanita introduced him to her mother. "Mom, this is Billy Roy."

He smiled, nodded his head and said, "Good evening, Mrs. Hemstead." He put his hand out to shake hers, but she totally ignored it.

Looking him up and down, Juanita's mother said, "So, you're a deputy sheriff."

"Yes, ma'am," he said with pride.

"Are you married?"

"No, ma'am."

"Do you have any girlfriends?" She listened intently for the answer.

Billy Roy was taken aback by this question, but answered it honestly while looking straight back into her eyes, "No, ma'am."

"Hmmm," she said. "Well, how come you want to go out with my daughter?"

Continuing to keep his eyes on hers, he answered, "Because I like her…she's nice…and she's brave!"

The mother was a little shocked to hear him say her daughter was brave. No one else had ever said that. "Well, where do you plan to take her tonight?" She still kept that stern look on her face. Billy Roy felt himself starting to sweat.

"There's a good movie downtown that I thought we would go see, and then maybe go to the Dairy Queen afterward."

Juanita's mother could see that Billy Roy had strong convictions and wasn't going to be an easy target for her intimidation. Juanita started giving her a "hurry up" look. Mrs. Hemstead thought to herself, "It's not worth it." Then she started to smile. "Alright, you two go and have a good time."

Billy Roy smiled at her. "It was nice meeting you, ma'am," he said as he put his hand out to shake hers.

She looked at his hand then slowly put her hand in his and shook it. "Be careful!" She said as she looked him straight in the eye.

"Yes, ma'am," he said as she let go of his hand.

Billy Roy opened the door and helped Juanita down the front steps and out to the car. "She's a very nice lady," he said wiping the sweat from his brow.

"Trust me, you got out light, Billy Roy," she said with a chuckle.

Halfway through the movie, Billy Roy took Juanita's hand. She looked at him with a smile that showed a little bit of shyness, but she let him hold her hand for the rest of the movie.

"I'm so glad I passed her mother's test," he said to himself with a big smile of accomplishment. "I think I'm going to enjoy getting to know Juanita better."

CHAPTER ELEVEN

The next morning Juanita was talking with Bonnie, "Guess what? I had a movie date with Billy Roy last night!" She was grinning from ear-to-ear.

"Oh, how cool! Did he behave himself?" The girls laughed at the question.

"Now, you sound like my mother. Yes, he was a gentleman." They both chuckled again. "You know? Actually...I think I like him a lot." Juanita said with a bit of faraway look in her eyes.

Bonnie could see Juanita was focused on her thoughts at the moment. "I'm so glad you two are getting along so well. Everyone needs a real good friend in their lives."

"You're right," she said as she went to her desk and started working.

That afternoon, Billy Roy showed up at the end of his shift at his usual time. He went over to Juanita's desk to sign in. "Howdy, Miss Juanita," he said with a smile.

"Good afternoon, Deputy," she answered back with her eyes fixed on Billy Roy.

"I was thinking maybe you'd like to have dinner with me tomorrow night."

Juanita tried to control her excitement, "Oh, I'd love to, Billy Roy."

"Well good. I'll pick you up about six, would that be ok?"

"Absolutely. Thank you for asking me." By this time Bonnie, who had stepped out of her office to see what was going on, rolled her eyes and returned to her paperwork.

"Ah, will I need to be interviewed by your mom again?" He said rather sheepishly.

Juanita laughed, "No, you are ok in her book."

Billy Roy looked relieved. "Ok then, it's a date." He picked up his bag and walked out to the car with a big smile on his face. "I really think I'm gonna like this gal," he said to himself as he started up his car and drove off.

The next night, Billy Roy picked up Juanita and drove to a little restaurant located at the city limits. They had a wonderful meal and enjoyed talking about things they did as kids, as well as, things they look forward to doing in the future.

The conversation was starting to wind down, so Billy Roy paid the tab and escorted Juanita to the car. "Would you like to go out to the park for a little while? We can watch the little animals look for something to eat, and we can talk some more." He started the car.

"Sure, that sounds great to me. I'm not quite ready to go home yet anyway." She wondered what he had on his mind. "I guess I'll find out," she said to herself as they drove to the park.

There were a couple of other cars parked down from where Billy Roy stopped his car. Although she wanted to be alone with Billy Roy, she felt better knowing that if something bad happened she could holler for help, if needed.

They walked over to a park bench and sat there looking at the stars for a few minutes. Quietly...almost in a whisper, Billy Roy leaned over to Juanita and asked, "Do you like to fool around?"

She jumped back from him and responded, "Do you like hot coffee poured on your neck?"

Billy Roy sat up straight and nervously chuckled, "I believe that answered my question."

"Now wait a minute, don't misunderstand me," she said as she scooted closer to him on the bench. "There's a time and a place for everything. This might be the time, but it isn't the place." She put her hand in his and smiled as she looked into his eyes.

"Hmmm, I might have to think this one over." He said as she came closer to his face. "Would it be alright if I kissed you?"

"Sure," she purred...lips puckered. He leaned close and gave her a little peck on the cheek. She opened her eyes quickly and said, "Come here!" She grabbed him around the neck and pulled him up against her body. Then she gave him a kiss that took his breath away. "Now, that's a kiss," she said as she let go of his neck.

"Oh boy is it!" At this point he figured he might as well see how far she planned to go. "Would you like to see my house?"

She smiled her sweet, angelic smile and whispered, "I thought you'd never ask."

He jumped up off the bench and extended his hand to help her up. "Billy Roy, you've got to promise me something?"

"Ok, what is it?" He had no idea what she was about to ask.

"Just promise me you won't tell my mother." They both cracked up laughing as they walked back to the car...in anticipation of an interesting evening.

CHAPTER TWELVE

Deputy George Kindell was driving up county road 2676 when he saw a car ahead of him driving erratically. The car came too close to the vehicle in front of it and then whipped around ahead of it. He increased his speed and turned on his flashers, passing cars until he was behind the speeder. George turned on his siren. The car slowed down and pulled over to the edge of the road.

George pulled in behind him and called the office. "Bonnie, this is George. I need you to run a check on this license plate for me. He's been speeding. I'm going to get out and talk to the driver." He read the number to Bonnie, hung up the phone, and got out of the car with his ticket book.

He walked up to the car and noticed the young driver was giving him a strange look. "Sir, you were driving rather erratically and you were speeding. We're you going to an emergency?"

"No," said the driver.

"May I see your driver's license, please?" George was keeping a close eye on the driver's actions as the young man reached around into his hip pocket. Instead of bringing up his billfold, he brought a .9mm pistol. George jumped back when he saw it and reached for his own gun. The man fired a shot, missing George, then hit the gas pedal and sped off quickly, throwing gravel back at the squad car. George ran to get in his car and took off in fast pursuit of the vehicle.

He picked up his phone and called the office, "Bonnie, we have an evading arrest suspect who fired a shot at me. I am in pursuit at this time. We are headed down CR 2676."

Brick heard the call from George, and picked up the phone. "George, are you all right?"

"Yeah, I'm fine, Sheriff. I'm right behind him."

"Alright, stay on him. I'll get someone out there to help you. Do not try to arrest him yourself."

"Yes, Sir."

Brick immediately got on the line and called both the police and state troopers to inform them of the pursuit. As he hung up the phone, Bonnie came into his office. "Sheriff, I ran a check on that license plate and that is a stolen car. It was reported stolen this morning from a parking lot downtown."

"Ok, we'll get on it." Brick relayed that information to George and the other departments he had called. He reiterated that the man was armed and dangerous, and to approach with caution.

George stayed with the driver as the speeds exceeded 90 mph and climbed up to over 100 mph, when George noticed that a car was pulling out in front of the stolen car. To keep from hitting the car, the thief quickly pulled to the other side of the road to miss it. Unfortunately it caused the stolen car to leave the road and slide off into the ditch. It came to rest against a large tree. George quickly pulled over with his lights flashing. He saw a state trooper pull off the road behind him. The two officers got out of their cars and approached the accident.

The man inside the damaged car slowly got out and appeared to be injured. He still had his pistol in his hand. The two officers, with guns drawn, told him to put down the pistol.

"Naw, if I do you'll arrest me, and I'll go back to prison. I'm not going back." He swung around and pointed his pistol at the officers. George and the trooper quickly ducked behind two nearby trees.

George shouted, "Put your gun down, now!" The man ignored the order and started shooting. Both officers opened fire on the man hitting him in the chest. He dropped his gun as he fell to the ground clutching his chest. They cautiously walked over to him. He was lying on his back and wasn't in any condition to be giving them any more trouble. George kicked the gun out of the man's reach and bent down a little to hear what the man was saying? "What did you say?"

The man looked up at George, with blood dripping from his lips, he whispered with his last breath, "Thanks." And then his body went limp.

George, staring at the body muttered to himself, "What?"

The trooper walked up at that moment, "What did he say?"

"He just said thanks," replied George as he stood up. Neither man spoke for a few seconds. The question "Why did he say thanks?" ran through their minds.

Finally the trooper said, "Let's get the ambulance and coroner out here and finish this up. Why don't you let the sheriff know what's going on while I make the other calls." George nodded as both men retrieved their phones from their pockets and made the calls.

Later, after the body was removed and the crime scene cleaned up, the men left to check-in at their respective offices.

Back at the sheriff's office, as George recounted what had happened, Brick looked at him and said, "You know what George? It appears it was another case of police suicide. The man wanted you to kill him."

George hung his head, "Geeze, I feel so bad..."

Bonnie, who had been standing in the doorway, chimed in, "I've been checking on him and found out his name was Eddie Simpson. He was thirty-eight, and did not have a job. He was divorced with no children. He had cancer real bad and didn't have the money to get it taken care of, and that's probably why he did what he did."

George shook his head slowly, "I just feel so bad."

Brick could see the pain in George's face. He got up out of his chair and went over to pat George on the shoulder. "George, I'll tell you what, you've had a rough, rough day. I want you to go home...take a couple of days off...go fishing or something. Do you like to fish?"

"Oh, yeah, I used to fish a lot up in Michigan. My wife does, too." Brick's kindness seemed to lift George's spirits a little.

"Do you have your equipment?"

"Yes, we sure do."

"I'm gonna call Sally. She has a fair size lake out in the country about ten miles from here. She owns the property around it. I understand you can do some good fishing out there. Why don't you and your wife pack up a lunch and go out there tomorrow."

"Well, I may do that, Sheriff. Thanks. I'll go talk to Gloria about it. And I've got a couple of days off with pay?" George's spirit seemed to lift as he thought about Brick's suggestion.

"Yeah, you deserve it." Brick was pleased that George was going to take him up on the offer.

"Ok, thanks again. I'll see you in a couple of days." George finished filling out his report on the incident and then left for home.

The next day George and Gloria set out to go to the lake on Sally's land. They had restrung their fishing reels, because the line was getting old. They really were looking forward to going out and relaxing. As they drove onto the property, they noticed that thick woods were all around the lake. Gloria was so excited, "Oh, George. This is just great! It kinda reminds me of Michigan."

"Yeah, it sure does." He was so happy that Gloria was enjoying the moment.

George stopped the car under a big tree to shade it from the Texas sun. They unloaded the car and carried the picnic basket and fishing rods to a group of trees close to where they would be fishing. They left the basket and blanket there and took the rods down to the water. George was in shorts and a t-shirt, and Gloria also wore shorts with a thin blouse. They both wore scruffy, old shoes because they knew they'd be getting muddy or wet.

George was the first to hook a fish. It was a nice size bass. "Hey, Gloria, look. I snagged a big bass." He was reeling it in when the fish got off the hook and swam away. "Ah, crap."

Gloria couldn't hold back from laughing as she watched George. "It's ok, Honey. We're going to throw them back anyway." She put a plastic worm on her hook and cast it into the water. Within a couple of minutes, she too had a fish on the line. She was able to land hers, though. It appeared to be about two pounds. She was excited, "See, I did it!" George was a little humbled by her first catch, but told her what a great job she did as he unhooked the fish and threw it back into the water.

They walked around the lake throwing their lines in hoping to catch the big one. Although they caught several during the morning, none of the fish were exceedingly large. All the same, they had a very relaxing morning. It was getting close to noon when they decided to stop and have some lunch.

George helped Gloria lay the blanket on the ground then Gloria began to unpack the picnic basket. There were thick chicken sandwiches with slices of tomato, potato chips, and frosty cans of coke. They sat on the blanket and enjoyed the meal as they watched the birds fly onto the tree limbs above their heads. The stillness of the moment brought peace to both of them as they finished their lunch. George said, "I feel so relaxed. In fact, this is the most relaxed I've been since we moved to Texas." Gloria smiled and nodded her head. "I guess we just needed to go fishing, didn't we?"

"I guess you're right, Sweetie. I am enjoying this, too. You know, it seems the bass are bigger here in Texas than they are back home." She finished putting the lunch items back in the basket and sat down next to George on the blanket.

George laughed, "Honey, everything's bigger in Texas."

Gloria took George's hand. "You know, I've been thinking. We talked about starting a family once we got settled in Texas, and I think maybe it's getting about that time. What do you think?"

George looked into her beautiful, green eyes and smiled, "I've been thinking about the same thing. I think we should start trying."

George watched as Gloria removed her shirt and shorts then leaned over and wrapped her arms around his neck pulling him down to her as she slowly leaned back onto the blanket. "This is a nice, quiet place. Don't you think we could start now?" She gave him a passionate kiss. He used his hands to search her body as the cooing of a dove was heard in the distance.

CHAPTER THIRTEEN

Brick and Sally were enjoying lunch in the café watching the leaves fall from the big pecan tree growing just outside the north window. Autumn in Texas is not like it is in the northern states where the beautiful, colorful leaves fall from September through October. The leaves in Texas are not real colorful. Most turn brown or dark red, and they usually fall at the end of October and through November. However, watching leaves fall no matter where you are can be an enjoyable experience.

Sally was so glad that Brick wanted to come for lunch with her. The time they spent together was always a treasure for her. She smiled as she looked out the window.

"You know Sally, tomorrow I'm going to take the day off and drive over to Louisiana to the casino. Would you like to go?"

"I've never been to a casino, but I must confess I've always thought it would be fun. I really don't have that kind of money to lose, though."

"Here's the thing," Brick explained. "Never gamble more than you can afford to lose."

"Well, that makes sense," she chuckled as she finished eating her sandwich. "What do you play there?"

"I generally play craps."

"Could I learn how to do that?"

Brick was excited that Sally seemed to be interested in going. "Sure, I can show you tomorrow. We'll leave here about six in the morning, go over and spend the day then leave about four which will get us home between nine and ten. It makes for a long day, but it'll be fun."

"Oh my…well…why not!" She had a big smile on her face as she looked at Brick. "I'm looking forward to spending the day with you."

They finished eating, and Sally started clearing the table. "Alright, I'll see ya in the morning, Sally." They waved to each other as he left the café to go back to work.

Brick headed back to the office, and let the girls know that he would be taking the next day off. They could tell he was excited about something, but decided not to ask, even though they were dying to know. Brick also called his deputies and informed them that he would be out of the office for the next day, but to call him on his cell, if necessary.

Five o'clock came early the next morning. Brick turned off the alarm just as Red jumped up and put his two front feet on the side of the bed. "Hey, boy, you ready to get up?" Red's tongue was hanging out of his big smile as Brick petted his head. I gotta pick up Miss Sally in a little while." Brick climbed out of bed, put his robe on and let Red out into the back yard. Red spotted a squirrel and tore out after him, barking all the way. Brick laughed and went back in the house to get ready for the long day ahead.

It was exactly six o'clock when he pulled up at Sally's house. He honked the horn twice. Sally came out and got in the truck. "Are we ready to go on our big adventure?" She said excitedly.

"That's the way to look at it girl. Let's go." He backed out of the driveway, pulled out onto the street and headed for FM 471 south.

"It's a beautiful morning," Brick said as he turned onto US 90 and headed east to Interstate 10 which would take them to Louisiana.

"Yes, it is," Sally said as she leaned back in her seat, enjoying the ride. "Now, I believe you were going to tell me how to play."

"Yeah, what you want to do is of course win."

His response made Sally laugh. "Yeah, that's the best idea."

"Anyway, we're gonna play with caution. Just play the inside numbers, that's five, six, eight, and nine."

Sally was confused already. "Ok, why do they call them inside?"

"Because that's what they are...inside the two, three, four, ten, eleven and twelve. We'll just play it easy and try not to make a killing."

Sally was more lost now than before she asked the question. "Ok, fine." She said as she rolled her eyes and continued to watch out of the window at the autumn scenery.

It was about eleven o'clock when they arrived in Louisiana. Brick drove up to the front of the casino for valet parking. The valet gave him his ticket, and Brick took Sally to the buffet. She was surprised at all of the delicious meats and vegetables she had to choose from. Brick selected ham, potatoes, and lots of vegetables. Sally had fried shrimp, shrimp cocktail and vegetables. "This is wonderful," she said as she put her plate on the table and sat down in the chair.

"Oh, this is nothing. Wait 'til you see all of the desserts. You'll have a hard time choosing what you want, I guarantee you." He smiled as he took another bite of ham.

They finished their lunch and Brick asked, "How about some dessert?" He was already up out of his seat and ready to survey the dessert area.

Sally put her napkin on the table and stood up. "What do they have?" She asked as he led her to the dessert buffet.

"Just about everything," he said with a big smile. They wandered along the buffet counter where the desserts were displayed. Brick took a piece of his favorite pecan pie topped with vanilla ice cream. He looked at Sally, "What about you?" He tempted her by putting the pie close to her nose.

She waved him off, "I really shouldn't... but....alright, let me see which dessert I can't live without." She chuckled as she watched Brick walk back to the table and dig into his pie.

As they left the restaurant Sally said, "I don't think I'll ever eat again. I'm so full."

Brick said, "Well, you ate three desserts, so I can understand why."

Sally popped him on the arm, "I did not! I only had two." They both laughed as she put her arm through his, and he led her into the casino.

Brick took her to the crap table where he bought in for $300. He told Sally, "Don't you buy in, we'll just use these chips."

"Alright," she said, looking around and taking it all in.

So Brick showed her how to place bets on the six and eight. She was a little hesitant to put chips out there. She kept trying to put a dollar chip out. "I'm sorry ma'am, you can't play just a dollar chip," the pit boss told her politely.

Brick saw that she was lost at this point and stepped in. "You have to put a minimum of six dollars on the six and eight. Everything else is a minimum of five dollars."

Sally looked at Brick and said, "Oh. Ok, thanks." She put six chips out and watched the dice roll.

They played and won a few points and lost a few points. Brick kept trying to teach her. He said, "Now remember the main thing is don't spend more than you can afford to lose. So we can afford to lose this. If we lose that, we're done. If we can win, that's good."

They didn't win any money, but they didn't lose much either. Finally Brick said, "Well, let's cash in and go play the slots."

Sally gave a sigh of relief, "Ok great. I really didn't enjoy playing craps, but I've heard slot games are lots of fun."

Brick responded, "I don't really play the slots that much 'cause I think you lose your money there, but we'll go do it for entertainment." Brick wanted Sally to have a good time, no matter what they did. He was getting to the point in their relationship to where he really didn't want to be without her, and her happiness was all he wanted.

They cashed in their chips and got one hundred and eighty dollars back. "We lost one hundred and twenty dollars." Brick said as they walked through the slot machines looking for one they wanted to play.

"Let's try this one!" Sally stopped and sat down on the stool in front of a machine in front of her.

Brick sat at the machine next to her and handed her a couple of twenty dollar bills. "I can't take that," she said as she reached into her purse. "I have my own money." She pulled out a one hundred dollar bill, "I can afford to lose a hundred dollars."

Brick laughed, "Ok, have at it." He put some money in the machine in front of him and started to play.

After about two hours of playing on several different machines and not winning much, Sally started getting bored. "Are you ready to go, Brick?"

"Let me play one more time." He pulled the handle and won a jackpot…three of a kind for two hundred fifty dollars. "Oh man, I hit it!"

"You sure did!" Sally was excited. "So how much money ahead are you?"

"Well, let's see." Brick started counting. "I'm two hundred seventy dollars ahead."

"Oh, Brick, that's great!"

"So, how did you come out?" Brick asked as he got up from the machine.

Sally looked in her billfold. "I've got eighty dollars left."

"So, it cost you twenty dollars. That's not bad."

"No, it's not bad at all. I really had a great time, Brick. Thanks."

They walked to the valet to get the truck. "That was fun." She had a big smile on her face.

"Yes, it was," he agreed as the valet brought the truck around. Brick opened the door for Sally to get in. "Let's go back to Texas." They both chuckled as he got in and took off down the highway.

Later as they arrived at Sally's place, she asked Brick if he wanted to come in.

"Naw, I'm kinda worn out after that trip. I think I'm gonna head back home and see what Red is up to."

"Yeah, I'm kinda tired myself, but it really was a lot of fun, Brick!"

Brick helped her out of the truck and said, "Well, I'll see you tomorrow, baby." Sally gave him a warm, passionate kiss then waved good bye as she walked up to her front door, unlocked it and went into the house. Brick got in his truck and left.

"What a wonderful day," she said as she locked the front door. Charlie ran up to her wagging his tail. It was obvious he was ready to go outside. "Come on, Charlie. Let's see what's going on in the back yard."

Brick drove into his driveway, turned off the motor and got out. As he entered the door to his house, Red ran up to him excited to see his master. "Ok, Red. Let's go." He opened the back door to let the happy dog out. As he watched the beautiful setter run around the yard, his mind took him back to the day he just spent with Sally and the kiss. "Dang, that gal has me hooked." He laughed as he joined Red out in the yard.

CHAPTER FOURTEEN

The bright, morning sun was already streaming through the windows in Brick's bedroom when the alarm went off. "Damn... I'm not ready to get up." He hit the snooze button and pulled the covers over him again. However, Red had other plans for Brick. He jumped up on the side of the bed where Brick was just drifting off to sleep and barked. Brick sat up quickly. "Crap, Red!" The dog was wagging his tail, letting Brick know he was ready to get up and play. "Alright, alright. Come on," Brick said as he yawned and got out of bed. He was exhausted after driving all the way to Louisiana and back again the day before. He went to let the dog out, then came back to get ready for work.

While he was getting dressed, he couldn't stop thinking about the great fun he had with Sally the previous day. "I wonder how things would have turned out if we had married right out of high school." He tried to envision this as he finished getting ready and headed to the kitchen to fix breakfast for himself and Red.

Brick didn't have the energy to take Red for his daily morning exercise on his land in the country, so after breakfast he gave Red a milk bone, petted him for a minute and left for work.

He arrived just before eight o'clock and was glad to see that Juanita was already there and had a fresh pot of coffee ready. Brick said, "Good morning, Juanita, is there anything I need to know about yesterday?"

"Naw, it was real quiet Sheriff. Oh yeah, there was one note there I left for you. A man named Fred Whitaker wanted to talk to you. I took his phone number. He said it was nothing that couldn't wait. He just wanted to talk to you."

"OK, I'll call him while I'm having my coffee." Brick poured himself a cup, went into his office and called Mr. Whitaker."

"Hello?"

"Hello, this is Sheriff Walls. You wanted to talk to me?"

"Yes, Sir. Thanks for calling back, Sheriff. When I go outside on my property, I can smell something strange. I'm not saying there's anything wrong, I'm just curious what it might be. I was wondering if you could come out to my place."

"OK Mr. Whitaker, I'll try to make it out right after one o'clock. How's that?"

"That would be great! Appreciate it sheriff."

"No problem. I'll see ya then about one o'clock." Brick hung up the phone. "I wonder what's going on out there. We'll I guess I'd better go out and see. It doesn't sound too earth shaking."

Brick finished up his morning duties and told Juanita, "I'll be gone after lunch. I'll be at Mr. Whitaker's. If you need me just give me a call on my phone."

Brick left and met Sally at the café for lunch. He and Sally discussed the previous day's events and Sally said, "I think playing craps is fun, but I think I like slots better because it's much easier to just pull the handle."

"Well, I guess that's ok, too."

After they had lunch, as Brick was getting ready to leave, he said to Sally, "I'm going to be gone out to the country for a while to Mr. Whitaker's. Do you happen to know him?"

"No, I can't say as I do."

"Well, I'm going out there because he has something he wants me to look at. I'll see you this evening. Ok? We'll find something to do when I finish work."

"I'm for it. Come out to my house for supper?"

"Sounds good to me. How about six-thirty?"

"It'll be ready."

"Any problem and I'll call you." He kissed her and left the café, got into his patrol car and headed out to Mr. Whitaker's. It was about a five mile drive. Whitaker's house was sitting back a ways from the highway. There were houses on each side of the house. Brick parked in the driveway, got out, looked around then, went up to knock on the door.

A rather heavy set man who looked to be about sixty came to the door. Brick said, "Mr. Whitaker?"

"Yeah, Sheriff, I'm Fred Whitaker. Come on in. I appreciate your coming by."

"What's this about a smell?"

"There's something out behind the house." Fred started walking to the kitchen straight to the back door. Brick followed cautiously with his hand over his revolver, not knowing what Fred had in mind. "Sheriff, can you smell something kinda odd?"

Sheriff smelled. "Yes, it's definitely some kind of strange odor."

"Well, I think that Johnny Boles, who lives there on the other side of me, is making drugs. This funny smell comes about twice a week and it just seems to me that someone is cooking something real acidic."

The sheriff smelled again and said, "I'm not an expert, but it does smell like somebody's making meth. Well, Mr. Whitaker, I'll certainly look into this."

"I don't want to cause any trouble, Sheriff. I just don't want to see anyone making drugs and getting kids hooked on the drugs they make. Ya know?"

"I understand, Sir. You're not causing trouble for anybody."

"Also, I don't want him to know that I was the one who called about this."

"No, no, Mr. Whitaker, your name will not be mentioned." Brick shook Whitaker's hand and said, "I appreciate your letting me know. We'll investigate this. Thank you for giving me a call."

With that Brick got into his car, drove back to the office, and called the local police department. "Is Jack Anderson available?"

"Just a moment, please." Jack was the head of drug enforcement for the city.

"This is Officer Anderson. Who is this?"

"Hi, Jack, this is Sheriff Walls. I just had a call from a fella that believes that someone in the house next to his is manufacturing meth. I wanted to get you in on it to tell me if you think that's the case, or is some lady just cooking a bad stew."

Jack laughed, "Ok, when do you want to do that?"

"Well, how about right now?"

"Where do you want to meet?"

Brick said, "I'll come by and pick you up. How about that?"

"Sounds fine. See you in a few minutes."

Brick told Juanita he'd be out of the office for a while and to call him if needed. He decided to use his truck, since he would be working undercover, and drove to the police station to pick up Jack.

Jack was coming out of the building when Brick arrived. He got into the truck, they shook hands, and Brick explained to him what he knew regarding the situation. "Ok, well let's go check it out," Jack said.

They arrived at the Whitaker house and went up to the front door. Fred Whitaker let them in. Brick introduced Jack and explained why they were there then they went out into the back yard. Jack took a big whiff of the air. "Oh, yeah. That's definitely meth being cooked."

"So I'm right. It is drugs," Fred said rather astounded.

"Yes, sir. You are right."

"What do you think, Jack?" Brick asked. "Should we go bust it up now?" Brick was letting Jack call the shots.

Jack replied, "I only see one car over there so I think the two of us can handle it." They got in the truck and moved it onto the street by the neighbor's driveway so that Fred would not be suspected of being the snitch. They got out of the truck and carefully surveyed the front of the property. The garage door was up a little and the smell seemed to be coming from inside. Jack motioned to Brick to move to the left side of the door while he positioned himself on the right side. They drew their guns, then, with their free hand they quickly pulled up the garage door.

The smell was overpowering as they stepped into the garage and noticed one man by a cooker. "Police," Jack hollered. "Put your hands up in the air. You're under arrest for manufacturing drugs."

The man was totally surprised to see Jack and Brick with their guns drawn. "What the..." Brick was getting the handcuffs ready to put on the suspect, as Jack continued to point his gun at him. As soon as the handcuffs were on, Jack turned off the burners. As they looked around they saw a large quantity of drugs already packaged and ready to be distributed. They searched the prisoner's pockets and found $1100 in ten and five dollar bills.

Brick led him into the house so that they could continue their investigation. Upon entering they found more cash, plus cocaine and marijuana. It was obvious he was an active distributor of drugs.

"What's your name?" Jack asked.

The man gave Jack a sharp look, "Johnny."

"Johnny what?"

"Just Johnny....I ain't talking," he growled.

"Well, Johnny, does anyone else live here?"

"Naw..."

"Really? I noticed some female clothing in the other room. Do you dress in female clothing?" Jack said with a smile.

"No, I don't." It was evident that Jack was irritating him, and Johnny didn't like it. "My girlfriend comes by once in a while.

"She doesn't live here?" Jack knew that his questioning was getting to Johnny so he continued to prime the pump.

"Naw, she just comes by."

Jack responded, "Then why are her clothes here?"

"She stays once in a while."

"What's her name?"

"I don't know." Johnny was obviously not going to give Jack anymore information.

"You don't know your girlfriend's name?"

"I ain't talking. I want a lawyer."

"Ok, we're gonna see you get a lawyer." With that, Jack got on his cell phone and called the police station. "This is Jack. I need a couple of officers. We have a fairly large drug bust here." He gave the address of the house then hung up.

He turned to Brick, "If you need to leave and get back to your office, I'll be ok here until the officers arrive."

Brick shook his head, "Naw, I'll stay with you until they get here."

Johnny was getting antsy, "How am I gonna get a lawyer?" He tried to get up, but Brick forced him back down into his chair.

"Just sit down and be quiet." Brick said sarcastically, "When you get to the station you can call all the lawyers you want, but you can only use one."

Johnny was not amused. He snarled at Brick and said, "I wish you'd undo these cuffs. I'd take care of you two."

"Oh, so you're a tough guy, huh?" Jack said. "Tough guys usually get harsher sentences than those who cooperate. Didn't you know that?"

"Fuck you," Johnny said trying to get the cuffs off his hands.

"Ok, you just sit back there and shut up," said Jack. He heard a vehicle pull up in the driveway and glanced out the front window to see if it was the officers. "It's not them."

Brick said, "Since I have on my uniform, why don't you go out in the garage and see who it is. I'll stay here with him."

"Ok," Jack said as he went into the garage. He saw a young man getting out of the truck. He was unshaven and looked to be in his late 20s or early 30s.

The man smiled at Jack, "Hey, where's Johnny?"

Jack responded, "Ah, he's busy right now. Whatcha need?"

"I'm supposed to pick up six hundred dollars worth of merchandise."

"Merchandise?" Jack asked.

The man looked at Jack curiously. "Yeah."

"Oh, ok. So what kind do you need?"

"Ah, three hundred fifty dollars worth of cocaine, and I need about thirty bags of marijuana. What did you say Johnny was doing?" He still wasn't sure he could trust this guy.

"Ok, wait right here and I'll get your stuff for you." The man nodded as Jack went back into the house. He looked through the drugs that were stacked in a room just inside the door. He was careful to make sure that Johnny didn't see him as he didn't want him to holler and scare the guy off.

Jack went back out into the garage carrying the drugs. "Where do you want me to put these?"

The man was walking toward his truck. "Right here in the front seat would be fine," he said as he reached into his billfold. "Do I need to pay for these right now?"

"Yeah, that'll be five hundred and ninety dollars."

The man handed six hundred dollar bills to Jack who reached into his pocket pretending to get the man his change. Instead, he pulled out his revolver, pointed it to the man and said, "You're under arrest."

The man's eyes got big as he stared at the gun pointed at him. "What do you mean I'm under arrest? You ain't a cop are ya?"

Jack smiled as he kept his eyes on the man. "It just so happens that I am."

74

"God dang, how the ...."

He started carrying on, and Jack said, "Never mind...just put your hands behind your back." Jack slapped the cuffs on him. "Come on," Jack said as he started pulling him back to the garage and into the house.

As they walked into the living room where Johnny and Brick were, Brick said, "Oh, we have company huh?"

The man with Jack shouted, "Damn, Johnny, why didn't you tell me you son-of-a-bitch!"

Johnny hollered back, "Do I look like I'm in any condition to let you know anything, Charlie?"

"Alright, that's enough," Jack said as he observed the patrol car pulling up to the house. Two officers got out and approached the house. Officer James Green was tall and about forty five. Officer Ronnie Pearson was shorter and younger than Green. Both came into the garage just as Jack and Brick were escorting the two prisoners out of the house.

"Well, looks like you've got quite a thing going here," Officer Green said as he looked around the garage and saw the drug manufacturing paraphernalia.

Jack said, "Yeah, James, I think we've busted up a pretty big operation here."

"And I see you have another one here," James said pointing to the man who made the purchase.

"Yes, he just showed up and wanted to go along with our party."

"Like hell, I did," said Charlie as he gave Johnny an "I'll get you later" look. The officers chuckled as they took the two men out to the squad car and down to the station to be booked.

A short while later, the investigator showed up in the police van. He took pictures and dusted for fingerprints. When he was finished, Jack and Brick helped him move all of the drugs and paraphernalia out to the van. They put up yellow "do not enter" strips around the house and locked it.

As the van was ready to leave, Jack turned to Brick, shook his hand and said, "Well, Sheriff, I certainly appreciate your cooperation and help on this."

Brick said, "It's been my pleasure. If you need anything from me, or when you need me to testify, just let me know."

"I'll do that. Thanks again," he waved as he got into the van. Brick pulled down the garage door, got into his truck and drove back to his office.

CHAPTER FIFTEEN

Deputy Sam Atkins was working the late night shift, patrolling the housing developments located in the county and looking for anything suspicious. Everything seemed to be in order. Most of the people had probably turned in for the night, since no lights were on in many of the houses. "Looks like it's going to be a quiet night," Sam said as he reached over to turn on his favorite radio station. However, just before he turned up the sound, he thought he heard a child crying. He turned off the radio, pulled over and rolled down his window. Sure enough, it was a child's voice.

"What in the..." he said to himself as he turned off the car and got out to look for the source of the noise. Sam used his flashlight to see, and cautiously started walking toward the area where he thought he heard the noise. He called out, "Who's out here?" He stopped to see if he could hear an answer. He heard nothing. "Who's out here?" He asked again.

As he moved the flash light around hoping to find something, he thought he heard a small voice. "Me." Sam saw a little figure wearing pajamas come out from behind a tree growing in the yard next to where he was standing. It was a little boy about three or four years old carrying a small kitten in his arms. The child was very hesitant to come any closer to Sam, so Sam dropped to his knees and started talking to the little boy to gain his confidence.

"Hi. My name is Deputy Sam. What's yours?"

The boy hesitated for a few seconds then responded, "I'm Paulo."

"Well, hi, Paulo. Why are you out here in the dark?"

The little boy was still hesitant, but answered Sam's question. "Fluffy was still outside when I woke up to go to the bathroom, so I came out to get him. He ran away from me, and I had to chase him. I got lost after I found him." He hugged the kitten tight.

"Do you live in one of these houses?" He was hoping that the child knew where he lived so he could get him back to his family.

"Yes," he answered quietly.

"Which one is your house?"

"I don't know," the boy said as he started to cry. The kitten in his arms was starting to fight Paulo to get down.

"Paulo, can I help you with the kitten?"

Sam got up and started to walk slowly toward the boy, keeping a friendly and non-threatening smile on his face. When he got about two feet from Paulo, he put his flashlight on the ground and slowly lifted the kitten from the boy's arms. It wiggled around, but finally settled down in Sam's arm hold. "Paulo, I'm a sheriff's deputy, and I'm here to protect you."

"Ok," Paulo said as he looked up to Sam.

"Why don't you pick up the flashlight and show us where the car is, so we can put the kitten inside while we look for your house. Ok?" Sam thought if he gave the child a little job it might make him feel better.

Paulo reached down and picked up the flashlight, shining it on the car. They walked to the car, put the kitten in the back seat and closed the door. Because of the late hour, Sam would not be able to go knocking on front doors looking for Paulo's parents. He knew he'd have to get some information from the child before he could locate his home. "Now, what is your last name, Paulo?"

"Rodriguez. I want to go home now." He was getting nervous again.

"That is exactly what I'm trying to do is get you home. Are you sure you live in one of these houses?" Paulo nodded his head "yes". "Ok, I'm going to call the office and have the other deputy look up your house number on the computer. Do you know your father and mother's names?"

"Carla is my momma. My daddy is Ben, but he's not home. He's in the Army somewhere."

Sam cleared his throat to keep himself from getting emotional. "Ok, well I'll call the office, and they'll tell us where you live, so don't you worry." He smiled at Paulo. "Let's get in the car, because it's getting a little chilly out here, and I don't want you to catch a cold."

The kitten jumped into the front when Paulo sat down in his seat. It curled up in the child's lap and purred. Sam called the office and gave the deputy the information Paulo had given him. Within a couple of minutes, Sam had the address.

The Rodriguez house was not located on the street they were on. It was one street over. Sam surmised that Paulo got confused when he went searching for the kitten out the back door and through the back yard of the neighbor's house behind his.

"Ok, Paulo, let's go take you and Fluffy home." He started the car and pulled onto the street.

"You know where I live?" Paulo asked excitedly.

"Yes, sir. It's right around this corner and half way down the street." Paulo was watching out the window.

As Sam was pulling up to the house, Paulo recognized his home. "That's it. That's my house. I want to get out now." He started to take the seat belt off, but the kitten wouldn't move from his lap.

"Paulo, I'll come around to get you and Fluffy. Just wait there a minute."

Sam got out and went around to open the door. "Do you want me to take Fluffy?" He asked as he started to open the door carefully to keep the kitten from running out.

"Ok," said Paulo. He gave the kitten to him as Sam opened the door and helped Paulo out. He took the boy's hand and together they walked up to the front door. Sam had Paulo ring the door bell, and then they stood there waiting for someone to come to the door.

It took about five minutes before the light came on and a female voice said through the door, "Who is it?"

Sam was just going to speak when Paulo shouted, "It's me, Momma. It's Paulo."

"Oh my God," the woman said as she unlocked the door. She took the boy into her arms, "Paulo, what happened? Why were you outside?" Then she noticed Sam standing there with the kitten in his arms. "Oh, dear... I'm so sorry. Who are you and why did you have my boy?" Her mood changed from happy to cautious.

"Are you Carla Rodriguez?" Sam asked.

"Yes, and you are...?"

"My name is Sam Akins. I'm a deputy sheriff. I was driving down Elm Street, when I saw Paulo standing behind a tree with the kitten in his arms."

"Oh my God, he was over there?" She had a look of panic on her face as she asked, "But why, Paulo? What were you doing over there? You were supposed to be in bed."

"Momma, I got up to go to the bathroom and Fluffy wasn't in my room, so I went outside to find him, and I got lost, and I was scared..." He started to cry.

Carla stooped down and hugged him tightly. "It's ok, baby. It's ok. This nice man found you and brought you back." As she looked up at Sam she realized he was still holding the kitten. She stood up and reached out to get the animal then handed it to Paulo. "Here, Sweetie you and Fluffy go to bed, and I'll be in to tuck you in again in a minute."

"Ok, Momma, but can I give Officer Sam a hug first?"

She looked at Sam as if to ask if it was alright. He nodded his head. "Ok, but then get to bed."

Paulo went up to Sam, who had stooped down to give him a hug. "Thank you, Officer Sam for helping me find my house."

Sam replied, "You are very welcome, Paulo. But promise me you won't go wandering out in the dark anymore."

"Ok, I won't." Paulo gave him another quick hug and skipped off to bed, with the kitten hanging off his arm.

"I guess I don't need to tell you that this could have had a very different ending." Sam said to Carla.

She hung her head down, "Yes, sir. I'm so grateful that you found him. I don't know what I would do without him. My husband is stationed in Iraq right now, and …" She started crying. "I guess I forgot to lock the door. I will never do that again. Oh, thank you so much, Sir. Thank you so much." She put her arms around Sam and sobbed. Sam gave her a minute to let it out of her system, then took her by the shoulders and gently pushed her away from him.

"Are you going to be ok, now?"

"Yes, I'm sorry. I've just had so much stress lately. I can't thank you enough for saving my boy. I will talk with him about the danger he put himself in. You won't have to worry."

"Yes, Ma'am, I know you will. Well, good night," he said as he walked out of the house and back to his car.

As he drove down the street, he remembered that this was why he rejoined the department. He felt called to help the citizens of Medina County, and this is where he belonged.

CHAPTER SIXTEEN

Bonnie neatly stacked up the papers on her desk and left them for the next day. She grabbed her purse and sweater then said good bye to everyone as she went to the parking lot to get into her black mustang that she loved. It was a great car and just right for her. She drove to her apartment, went in and changed her clothes into something more casual, after which she went to the kitchen to fix dinner. Looking in her refrigerator she decided she didn't like what she saw. "This is not going to cut it," she said as she closed the door. "I might as well go to Sally's restaurant." She debated whether to drive or walk but decided it was probably better to walk to get the exercise she needed. When she was in the military police she got lots of exercise and she kind of missed it now. It was only about four blocks to the restaurant, so it was no big deal.

She left the house, locking the door behind her, and headed down the sidewalk to the restaurant. The air was refreshing, although it does remain very warm during autumn in Texas. She waved to a couple walking on the other side of the street. Bonnie was very glad she made the decision to walk. "It really is the simple things in life that make you smile," she said to herself as walked up to the restaurant and went in to find a table.

Sally saw Bonnie come in and went over to welcome her, "Hi, Bonnie. How are you doing?"

"I'm a little tired, to tell you the truth. I just walked up here from my house and I can tell I'm a little out of shape." Both ladies chuckled. "After I got home from the sheriff's office, I didn't feel like cooking dinner, so I decided to walk up here."

"Well, I'm so glad you did," Sally said as she handed Bonnie a menu.

Bonnie glanced quickly at the menu then said, "I think I'll have the roast beef with potatoes and green beans. Do you have gravy with it?"

"Yes, we do," Sally responded with her typical Sally smile.

"Great! And I'll have a piece of that delicious pecan pie for dessert," she said as she handed the menu back to Sally.

"Will that do it?" Sally asked as she took the menu.

"Oh, I'll have a glass of sweetened ice tea, too. Thanks, Sally."

"Ok, I'll put your order in, and I'll be right back." Bonnie leaned back in her chair, closed her eyes for a second, and took a deep breath.

Sally came and sat down at the table. Speaking in a quiet tone she said, "Bonnie, do you see that man over there at the table in the corner?"

Bonnie turned a bit to see a young man in his thirties, dressed in casual clothes with disheveled hair and a short, dark beard. "Yeah, I see him. He doesn't impress me much," she said as she turned back around facing Sally.

"Well, the other day when you came in for lunch, he asked me who you were and if you were married. He seemed interested in you."

"That's nice, but that's a one way street," Bonnie answered politely hoping that was the end of that conversation. About that time the man came over to the table.

"Sally, are you going to introduce me to this beautiful, young lady?" He said as he gave Bonnie a smile.

Feeling a bit uncomfortable Sally said, "Ah, yeah. Bonnie, this is Lester Finch. And Lester, this is Bonnie."

Lester grabbed Bonnie's hand and shook it. They both exchanged smiles. "Do you mind if I sit down here?" Not waiting for an answer, he pulled out the chair and sat next to Bonnie. He commenced with some small talk, and even though Bonnie was still not overly impressed by him, she managed to briefly answer the questions he asked.

The restaurant was getting busy, so Sally left the conversation to check on Bonnie's order and go wait on other customers. Within a few minutes she brought Bonnie her meal, hoping that Lester would leave. Unfortunately, he did not. He continued to converse while Bonnie tried to enjoy the wonderful food in front of her. "Please don't feel like you have to stay, if you have somewhere you're supposed to be." She said as she sipped her tea.

"Oh, no I don't have anywhere I need to be. I'm just enjoying sitting and talking with you." He said with a big smile.

"Swell," Bonnie thought to herself as she took another bite of food. Sally brought her the pecan pie she ordered and gave her an "I'm sorry" look. Bonnie just gave her a short smile and started to eat the pie. She had looked forward to savoring the flavor of her favorite pie, but instead, she just ate it quickly so she could pay the tab and leave.

Within a couple of minutes, Sally finished the pie and was ready to go. Lester was still talking as she looked at the tab, pulled out some money from her purse, left it on the table, then walked to the door with Lester beside her, still trying to make small talk. As they stepped outside, Lester asked, "Did you drive here?"

Bonnie answered, "No, I walked. I live fairly close." She really hesitated to say much more.

"Oh, great! Well, let me take you home." Lester saw this as an opportunity to really get to know her better.

"Thanks, but I need the exercise," Bonnie responded trying to be polite as she walked toward the sidewalk.

Lester persisted, "Oh, but you got the exercise walking here. You don't need to exercise after you eat. You need to let your dinner settle."

"No, that's okay. I'll be alright." Lester continued to press the issue as they reached the sidewalk. Hoping that it would put an end to this, Bonnie gave in and agreed to let him drive her home.

He led her to his car which was an old two-door Chevrolet. She proceeded to get in while he walked around to the driver's side door and got in. He turned to look at her and asked, "Now, where do you live?"

She told him, "Four blocks right up this street."

He started the car and the first thing he did was make a left-hand turn. "Oh, that's not the way, is it," he said. He drove around the block and kept talking to her. "Do you have anything planned for tonight?" he asked.

"Yes, I do," she replied. "I'm not available." Bonnie was regretting her decision to let him drive her home. Not only was she irritated at the situation, but she was also starting to get a little nervous about his demeanor.

"Well, how about tomorrow night?" It was obvious that he was not getting her message.

"No, I'm busy then, too." She kept her eyes fixed on the road ahead.

"Well, are you going to be busy all the time?"

"Very likely I am." She pointed to a building just ahead of them. "That's it," she said loudly.

He pulled over into the driveway, shut off the engine, and reached over to put his hand on her leg before Bonnie realized what he was doing. "I sure would like to see more of you," he said with a grin.

At this point, Bonnie had had enough. "Would you please take your hand off my leg," she said as she reached to open the door. Lester quickly reached across her and closed the passenger door before she had it opened all the way. Then, he ran his hand further up her leg. Bonnie took hold of his arm and in one quick twist had it behind his back in an excruciating, painful manner.

"Oh...oh God...let go of my arm!" He screamed.

"I'll let go of your arm when you quit putting your hand on my leg. And if you refuse, I can break your leg, your arm, or dislocate your shoulder. Which would you prefer?" Bonnie let her military training take over.

"Neither one...oh...let go of me! Damn you bitch...let go!" She gave it one little twist then reached over and opened her door. "Damn bitch, where'd you learn to do that?" He said as he rubbed his arm trying to relieve the pain.

"I told you I was in the MPs. Now, get your life straight fella. Fooling around like that...you're going to get yourself killed." She opened the door, got out, slammed the door, and went up to her apartment. Lester burned rubber getting away from the building.

Bonnie went inside, washed up and changed into her pajamas. She put the tea kettle on because she felt that a cup of hot tea might help to settle her nerves. As she waited for the kettle to whistle, she sat on the sofa to reflect on what had just happened. "What made me get in the car with that bastard? What was I thinking?" The tea kettle started whistling so she got up, fixed her tea and sat back on the sofa where she eventually drifted off to sleep.

The next morning she was at the office early and so was Juanita. She decided to share her experience with her. "Oh, my gosh, Bonnie. What was his name?"

"Lester."

Juanita could not help herself, "Oh, Lester the molester, huh?" They both cracked up laughing.

Brick walked in about that time, "What's so funny?"

The two looked at each other and Bonnie said, "Oh, we're just having a little girl talk."

"Well, I don't care to hear it. Get me some coffee when it's ready," he said as he went straight to his office and shut the door.

The girls looked at each other. "He's not in a very good mood this morning, is he?" Juanita said as she sat down at her desk. "By the way, have you got a boyfriend?"

"No, in the short time I've been here, I haven't found anyone that I'd care to date. However, there is a guy that works at the convenience store where I fill up. He's real cute, but I don't know anything about him. Next time I go in, I'm going to find out. How about you?" The coffee was finished brewing, so Bonnie went over to pour Brick a cup.

"Well, I had a steady boyfriend. We went to school together. He's was ok, but we never got real serious. I don't know, maybe someday Billy Roy and I might develop a long-term relationship. He's already found out that coffee isn't the only thing that gets hot with me." They both laughed as Bonnie knocked on Brick's office door and brought him his coffee.

"Sheriff, are you feeling alright this morning?" Bonnie said as she set the cup on his desk.

Brick looked up. As he picked up the cup he said, "I'm ok. I had a call from an old friend of mine this morning on the way to the office. It seems while his daughter was at Sally's café this morning, a man in his early 30's came to her table uninvited. He sat down and started asking questions about where she lived, where she worked, and if she drove herself to the café." Bonnie gulped. "It seems he was a real pain in the ass, and wouldn't leave her alone. He even put his hand on her leg under the table." Brick took a sip of coffee. "Anyway, my friend wanted me to find him and lock him up. He wasn't ready to file a complaint, though. I called George to go by and see if the guy was still there so he could talk to him, but he apparently had already left."

"What will you do when you find him?" Bonnie asked, contemplating whether or not she should share her story with Brick.

"Well, it's a sticky situation. Actually, until someone files a complaint, all we really can do is talk to this jerk and encourage him to leave town."

Bonnie decided to "let sleeping dogs lie". Not only did she not want to get Lester in trouble since she put herself into that situation, but she also didn't want Brick to know how stupid she was. "Well, enjoy your coffee," she said as she went back to her office.

CHAPTER SEVENTEEN

Sally arrived at the Sweet Pea Café at 7:30 a.m. She was pleased to see that many of the tables were full. Most of the customers were eating doughnuts, drinking coffee, and engaged in light conversations. She headed back to the work room and started to gather together the ingredients for her favorite pastry, Mike's German Chocolate Cake. She called it "Mike's" after a long time friend of hers who had given her the recipe for this delicious cake. Everyone who tried it liked it. She was delighted to have such a wonderful dessert to offer them. The restaurant was a favorite place in town, so Sally stayed busy all day.

Later, as the day was winding down, Sally realized that Brick hadn't been in during the day. "I wonder if everything is ok?" she thought. "If he's been that busy, he'll be too tired to fix himself something to eat. I'd better invite him to dinner this evening." She picked up the phone and dialed Brick's number.

As Brick was preparing to lock up for the day, the phone rang. "Now what?" He mumbled to himself as he answered the phone, "Sheriff Walls. How can I help you?"

"Hi, Brick." Brick recognized that sweet voice immediately.

"Oh, hi, Sally. How are you doing?" It was so nice to hear her voice at the end of a busy day.

"I'm great! How about you?" She sounded a little excited.

"I'm fine. I was just closing up for the night," he said as he placed the last file in the desk drawer.

"What are you gonna be doing this evening?" It was evident she had something in mind for him.

"Well, I guess I'll go get something to eat, watch some TV, and go to bed."

"Brick, would you like to come over for supper?"

"It sounds good to me. What time do you want me there?"

"Dinner will be ready at six o'clock."

"Ok, see you at about six then. Thanks for the invite, Sally!"

"Oh, you are so welcome, Brick. See you shortly."

Brick hung up the phone, "I'm sure looking forward to that dinner tonight, 'cause no one cooks a meal better than Sally. Maybe she'll have some of that German chocolate cake I like so much." Brick's mouth was watering by the time he closed the door to his office and left.

Red barked as Brick pulled into his driveway. "Howdy, Red...I'll be right there to feed you." He got out of the car and walked into the house. Red's tail was wagging fast, and he had a big smile on his face. He barked at Brick again. "Ok, ok...let's go outside," he said as he petted the big dog on the head and opened the back door. They liked to run and play catch with a tennis ball. After a few minutes, Brick walked back inside to get Red's food ready, while the big Irish setter continued to survey the back yard.

Brick laid the dog dish on the floor and called to Red, "Come on, Boy. I've got a dinner date tonight, and I have to get ready." Red came running through the doorway and went straight to his dish. Brick laughed, rubbed Red's head again, and went to get ready for the evening.

It was five fifty-five when Brick left the house and drove to Sally's place. It was only five minutes down the street. He pulled into her driveway, turned off the car, walked up to the front door and knocked.

Sally opened the door, "Hi, Brick," she said as she gave him a peck on the cheek and invited him in. He put his hat on the hat rack, then turned and asked, "Is there something I can do to help?"

"You can pour the wine. Would you like red wine or port?" Her smile was so alluring.

"I think a little red wine would be nice," he said as he followed Sally to the table.

"You pour the wine, and I'll get the dinner."

"What are we having," he asked as she walked into the kitchen.

"Poor Man's Swiss Steak," she answered from the kitchen.

"Hmm, I've eaten a lot of different food, but what is Poor Man's Swiss Steak?"

Sally was entering the dining room with a plate of meat that smelled terrific. Brick noticed the meat was covered in a creamy mushroom sauce. Sally also brought out a bowl of mashed potatoes and a bowl of green beans. She looked into Brick's eyes and said, "Now, Brick, a good cook never tells her secrets." They both chuckled as they sat down to eat. Brick raised his glass of wine and said, "A toast to a wonderful cook!" Sally looked deeply into Brick's eyes and took a sip of her wine.

After dinner, Brick helped Sally take the dishes to the kitchen. "Brick would you like to try a glass of chocolate wine?"

"Chocolate wine? I've never heard of it."

"It's really very tasty," she said as she took two clean glasses out of the cupboard, decanted the cork, and poured the wine. "Here, try it." She handed a glass to Brick.

He took a sip. "Hmm...it's actually very, very good!" They walked into the den and sat on the sofa together. Brick looked at Sally, "You know it's sort of like being married...sitting here, having a little wine after enjoying a great dinner. We've both been married...me for a very short time. She was 18 and I was

19. Neither one of us knew anything except desire. And you were married, too weren't you while I was in the service?"

Sally said, "You know, I had a big crush on you. When you got married it broke my heart. I stayed single for several years, and then I foolishly married David. I don't know what I was thinking. It was a disaster from the beginning. Remember during your senior year, when you and your buddies used to go play pool at the pool hall, and sometimes David would leave you a glass of beer when he left?"

Brick laughed out loud as his mind took him back to that time. "Yeah, we had fun."

"Well," Sally continued, "he became quite a drunkard. He was very possessive and everything had to be his way or the highway. He used to take it out on me if anything went wrong. It got to the point where I was afraid for my life. After nine months of his abuse, I finally had enough and asked him for a divorce. He told me he'd kill me before he'd ever give me a divorce. After that, he started to beat me, and it was only after interference of a neighbor who heard me crying, did he stop that night. I really believe my neighbor saved my life. The police came and arrested him for life endangerment. He was given five years in prison, but somehow he ended staying there ten years. When he got out, he tried to come to the house. I got a restraining order against him. He is not supposed to come near me or try to contact me again or he'll be put back in prison. I haven't heard from him since, and I'm finally starting to feel more comfortable now."

Brick was appalled at what he heard. He had no idea that David had become such a loser. "Sally, I'm so sorry you had to go through all of that."

"Yes, I know. It was foolish of me to think that it would ever work out, but it's over the dam now and done with."

"No, damn it, what he did was wrong, and if he ever contacts you, I pity his ass."

"Thank you, Brick, but I don't want you to get upset. It's all over now." Sally felt very protected and cared for at that moment, so she leaned over and gave Brick a big hug and a kiss on his cheek. "Let's watch a movie," she said as she walked over to the television. When she came back to the couch and sat down, Brick put his arm around her shoulders. They both smiled as the movie began.

When the movie was over, Brick turned to Sally and said, "Sally, I have really enjoyed this evening. I'd like to sit and talk some more, but I've got to get home. Work comes early in the morning." He rose from the couch and offered his hand to Sally to help her up.

Sally took hold of his hand, stood up and said, "Brick, I've had such a good time having you here. Would we be able to do this again?"

Brick looked in her beautiful blue eyes, "Of course, Sally. You just let me know, and I'll be here."

"Ok, will I see you tomorrow afternoon at the café?" It was obvious she didn't really want him to leave.

"Of course, I'll stop by." He put his arms around her and pulled her tight as they locked into a kiss.

When it was evident that this could lead to something more, Brick pulled away and said, "I'd better go." They walked to the door, and he gave her a quick peck on the cheek. "See ya tomorrow." He walked down the porch steps, got in his car, and drove away.

Sally waved and closed the door behind her. "What a wonderful evening," she said to herself as she went upstairs to get ready for bed.

CHAPTER EIGHTEEN

The following day, Sally decided to take the morning off from work to take care of some personal things and tidy up the house. She was busy sweeping the kitchen, when the phone rang. "Now who could that be," she wondered. "I'll bet that's Brick." She put the broom up against the kitchen wall and answered the phone, "Hello?"

A gravelly low voice spoke, "Hello, ya slut!"

"What?" Sally was totally taken a back. "Oh, my God! It can't be…"

"You know who this is."

"David, you're not supposed to be in touch with me." Her voice was shaky, "I'll call the police if you don't hang up now."

The voice continued, "Yeah, I just wanted you to know I haven't forgotten you. I promised you I'd kill you, and that promise stands." Sally was petrified by this time. "Be aware. Look over your shoulder. I'm going to kill you." With that, the phone went dead.

Sally immediately called Brick.

Brick sat down at his desk with a fresh cup of coffee. He had just got off the phone after listening to a man complaining about his neighbor's son practicing his drums late into the night. He decided to have Albert go by that night and check out the complaint. He took a sip of coffee just as the phone rang. "Damn it. What is it this time?" He mumbled to himself as he grabbed the phone. "Hello?"

"Oh, Brick, I'm so sorry to bother you, but I just got a call from David. He said he's going to kill me." Brick sat straight up in his chair. Sally continued, "I'm so scared, Brick!" She started to cry.

"It's gonna be ok, Sally. It's gonna be ok. Did he say where he was?" Brick asked as he started to pick up his keys off the desk and put his hat on.

"No, he didn't."

"Sally, I'm gonna have the deputy start a check on him. You stay right there and make sure all of the doors and windows are locked. I'll come over to check on you in a few minutes."

"Ok, Brick. Thank you so much. I just didn't know what to do." Sally started to cry again.

"Do what I said and I'll be there shortly. Bye, Sally."

"Bye, Brick." Sally hung up the phone and quietly walked around the house checking to make sure the doors and windows were locked, like Brick told her.

Brick immediately called Billy Roy to come back to the office. He was around the corner checking on a stalled car, so it only took a couple of minutes for him to arrive at the office. Billy Roy could tell that Brick had a sense of urgency in his voice, so he hurried into the building.

He was a little out of breath, "Yes, Sir. What do you need me to do?"

"Billy, I need you to run a check on this man for me." He briefly explained to Billy Roy how David had threatened Sally. "I need you to put an all points bulletin on him. I want to know where he is ....and soon!"

"Ok, Sheriff."

"I'm going over to Sally's house now to make sure she is ok. Call me as soon as you get any information on this guy."

Billy knew he'd better start trying to find this guy immediately. "Yes, Sir, I'll call you as soon as I find something."

Brick walked swiftly out the door and straight to his vehicle. He called Sally on the phone when he arrived, so she wouldn't be frightened when he knocked on the door.

He had just rung the door bell, when Sally quickly opened the door and pulled him into the house.

"Oh, Brick, how can I ever thank you? I'm so scared." Sally put her head on his shoulder and started to cry again.

Brick caressed her hair and tried to calm her down. "It's ok, Sally. I'll make sure you are safe. You won't be able to stay here tonight. I'll get you a room somewhere, or you can come and stay at my place for the night, but you're *not* going to stay here."

Sally looked up into Brick's eyes. "Oh, Brick, I don't know what to say. I'm so confused."

"Don't worry...we'll take care of you." His phone started ringing.

"Sheriff Walls."

"Sheriff, It's Billy Roy. Here's the information I've been able to come up with so far. We've got David Cosgrove, age 50, who was placed in Huntsville prison for aggravated assault. He served five years during which time he was given an additional five years for assaulting an officer. He was released a month and a half ago. We haven't located him yet, but we're still working on it. Anything else I can do?"

"No, that's it. Just keep working on it."

"Ok, Sheriff. Talk to you later." They both hung up.

"Well, that does it," Brick said. "You're going to come and stay with me, Sally, until we find out where this guy is and what he's up to. I'll feel much better if I know you're safe."

"Brick, I..I..I..ok, but I have my dog, Charlie, here."

Charlie was a very friendly English springer spaniel, and Sally was stroking his head as they talked. "That's not a problem. You know I have Red, and I'm sure they'll get along fine. If they don't, we'll put them in separate quarters, but I'm sure they'll be alright. Why don't you get some things together, and we'll head on over to my place."

Sally was reluctant, but she didn't really have any alternative at this point. "Well, alright," she agreed as she turned to go up the stairs and pack some things to take with her.

It wasn't long before she came down the stairs with a small suitcase. She went into the kitchen to get Charlie's dish and food, and then walked up to Brick. "You know, I probably ought to take my car, too in case I have to go somewhere while you're gone."

Brick thought for a moment then said, "Alright, that's a good idea. Let's go get in the cars. I'll follow you." Brick took the suitcase and dog food. Sally took the dog dish and the dog. She put the dog in her car, got in and drove to Brick's house.

Red was waiting at the door wagging his big tail. He was happy to see Brick, but when he saw Charlie, he stopped and cautiously checked him out. Red must have decided that Charlie was alright, because he barked, wagged his tail and started running through the house. Charlie took off behind him. Brick went to the back door to let them out in the yard.

"Sally, do you need to go into work later, or can they handle it without you?" Brick really didn't want her any place where David would find her, and especially not at the café.

"I'll call and tell them I'm not coming in today." Sally was trying to keep from totally falling apart.

"Good. I'll go back to the office and finish a couple of things. Maybe we can locate this scum bag and put him under arrest before I come home. Just stay here....read some magazines or watch TV... just don't go outside. Ok?"

"Yes, Brick.....oh, thank you so much." She forced a smile on her face and gave him a hug.

Brick left the house looking all around the area as he got into his car. He drove slowly to the office, watching for David. Unfortunately there was no sign of him.

When he walked into the office, he went immediately to see if Billy Roy had any more information. "How's the search going, Deputy?"

"I'm sorry we've checked the car rentals, license bureau, and several other places, but haven't come up with anything yet. Did she say where he was calling from?"

"No, she didn't know. Just keep trying to come up with some leads. Maybe Huntsville might have some information. Call 'em up."

"Yes, Sir." Billy Roy was looking up the phone number as Brick walked back into his office to finish up some paperwork.

It was only a few minutes before Billy Roy came back into Brick's office. "Sheriff, it seems that before David went to prison, he sold all his interests here in Maranda to pay his lawyers, and as far as we know, nobody has seen him since he left prison."

Brick was disappointed with the news, "Ok, you'd better get back out on patrol. Keep your eyes open. If you see anyone or anything strange around Sally's house or mine, let me know immediately. Thanks, Billy Roy."

"I'm happy to help. I just hope we can get this guy before he causes Miss Sally any more problems." He smiled and left the building.

Brick decided to check on Sally. He dialed his home phone number.

"Hello?" The voice on the phone was very cautious.

"Sally, it's me. How are you doing?"

"Hi Brick. Everything seems normal. The dogs are asleep right now, and I'm just cleaning up the house a bit."

Brick smiled, "Hey, you don't have to do that."

"Yes, I want to, and I'll have supper ready when you come home." Sally seemed pleased that she could help Brick in some small way.

"Well, that sounds great. Thank you, Sally. I'll see you about six o'clock." They said their goodbyes and hung up the phone.

The phone at Sally's house rang a few times. The person on the other end cursed and said, "I'll bet that bitch has skipped out on me, but I'll find her if it takes the rest of my life. And when I do, she'll suffer like I did the last ten years."

CHAPTER NINETEEN

Brick came home a little before six. The dogs were eager to play ball with him, so he hung his hat on the rack, picked up the ball and headed out to the back yard to play with them. The two dogs barked and chased the ball numerous times. Finally Brick called them over so he could rub their heads and talk to them.

While they were outside, a whiff of food fresh out of the oven reached Brick's nose, so he decided to go in to see what Sally was cooking. "M-m-m-m. That smells great!" He said as he walked into the kitchen.

"Well, I hope it tastes as good as it smells." Sally said as she put the dinner on the table.

"I'm sure it will," he said as he went to the bathroom to wash up.

She was just putting the last bowl on the table when Brick asked, "So, what's for supper?"

"We have fried chicken, black-eyed peas, mashed potatoes, and green glop."

Brick stopped, "Now that one's got me. What in the heck is green glop?"

Sally couldn't help laughing, "Well, come over here, and I'll explain it to you."

Brick sat down at the table eager to tear into that fried chicken. He filled his plate with chicken and the vegetables, but when he came to the green glop, he hesitated. "It looks like whipped cream to me." He looked at Sally inquisitively.

Sally couldn't help but chuckle as she watched Brick gingerly dip his spoon into the conglomeration. "Yes, it does have whipped cream in it, along with Jello pistachio pudding mix, crushed pineapple, and chopped pecans. You mix it altogether and let it chill thoroughly. You can use it as a salad or a dessert. So, what do you think?"

"Sounds delicious," Brick said as he slowly put a spoonful in his mouth. "M-m-m-m, it really *is* delicious but, I didn't have any of those ingredients here."

"Yes, I know. I slipped out to the store," Sally admitted.

Brick scowled at her, "I told you not to go out. I don't want anything to happen to you, Sally."

"I know. I know. I'm sorry. I just wanted dinner to be special for you. Do you forgive me?" She had a little girl look on her face. "Please?"

They both laughed and started eating their dinner.

When they finished, Brick helped Sally clear the table and wash the dishes. "Thanks, Brick, for helping," she said as she hung up the dish cloth.

"Hey, thank *you* for making this delicious meal. And thank you for introducing me to green glop!" They both chuckled again. "I can't wait to see what we'll have tomorrow."

They turned off the kitchen light and went out to the patio. They fed the dogs then sat down to enjoy the cool of the evening. "This is a very nice place, Brick," Sally said as she eased herself into the comfortably cushioned lounge chair.

"Thanks. My folks enjoyed it out here. It's nice to look at Mom's Garden and remember the good times we all had here, before they passed away."

"I know you miss them," she said looking into his eyes.

Brick sighed as he responded, "Yeah, I do."

Changing the subject, Sally said, "I noticed you don't park your truck in the garage. Why is that?"

"In there I have a 1960 Chevy convertible. I've wanted one for ages and ages, and I finally got one. I keep it covered in there to protect the finish. One of these days we'll go for a ride with the top down." He was smiling as he thought of getting the old car out and taking Sally for a spin.

"That sounds like lots of fun, Brick! I'd like to do that." It was so easy to talk with Brick. It was as if they were a married couple. Sally knew she was starting to fall in love with him, but she didn't want to rush in to anything. Besides, he was still getting over the loss of Helen, and she didn't want anything to get in the way of their happiness, especially the memory of a dead lover.

"Yes, we might do that one evening." Brick said as he adjusted his chair around to where he could see Sally better. "But right now I want you to stay under cover 'til we can find David and get him under control." Brick was very adamant.

"I suppose you're right. I won't go into the restaurant and café. I have good help there, and they can get along without me."

"Good idea. You just stay here, and we'll find him pretty soon."

A car drove slowly passed the front of Brick's house. The driver looked at the vehicles in the driveway. "That Chevy looks like the one she used to drive." He drove a little further down the street, turned around, came back and parked two houses down from Brick's house without being seen.

Sally asked Brick, as they watched the two dogs chasing some night bugs flying over their heads, "Did you get the mail when you came in this evening?"

"No, I forgot." Brick was laughing as the dogs bumped heads trying to catch the bugs flying above.

Seeing that Brick was having a good time watching the dogs' antics, Sally said, "I'll go get it for you." She got up, went through the house and out to the mailbox on the front porch.

Little did she know that two doors down, a man in a parked car was watching her. "That *is* her car. I knew it. This is where the bitch is!" After Sally went back in the house, David drove off down the street and onto Interstate 90. He pulled into a small motel and went in to register.

The clerk was pleasant, "How many nights, Sir?"

"Just one," replied David. As the clerk got the room key, David thought to himself, "It's only gonna take one night to get done what I came here to do." He took the key then got into his car. "Hell, I might as well find a bar and have a few drinks before I go have some fun."

Brick and Sally decided to come back in the house to watch their favorite television programs. After the ten o'clock news, Brick got up from the sofa and stretched. "I think it's time to let the dogs out and then get ready for bed." When he opened the back door, the dogs enthusiastically ran outside.

"Yes, I guess you're right." Sally felt a little uneasy at this point. After all, here she was in her ex-boyfriend's home, and they are talking about getting ready for bed.

She got up from the chair she was sitting in. "Good night, Brick," she said as she walked down the hall to the guest bedroom. Brick let the dogs back into the house then went into his bedroom. Red and Charlie laid down in front of the doors.

It was one-thirty when Charlie started whining outside Sally's bedroom door. She didn't want Charlie to wake up Brick, so she quickly got out of bed, and let him out the back door. He was only gone a few minutes when he came back to the door. Sally let him in, closed the door, and then went back to bed.

David looked at his watch and saw that it was almost two o'clock. He got up, paid the tab, left the bar and went to his car. In the glove box he found the revolver that he carried, even though he was a felon. He put the revolver in his pocket, got into the car, and drove to where he had seen Sally.

He pulled his car in front of Brick's house and looked it over carefully. He took the last sip from the whiskey bottle he kept under the seat, and quietly got out of the car.

David walked up onto the front porch and slowly tried the door handle. It was locked. He walked around the side of the house to the back gate, opened it, and slowly walked up the steps to the back door. He checked to see if it was unlocked...it was!! Sally had forgotten to lock the door when she let Charlie out earlier. Quietly opening the door, he went into the house. David carefully walked through the kitchen and to the hall where he figured the bedrooms were located.

It was very dark in the hall, and David had a hard time finding the doors. He eased down the hall to the first bedroom. As he reached out, he suddenly heard a low growl. He looked to his right and saw a big dog staring at him in a crouched position. The dog growled again. David swung his revolver around toward the dog when suddenly another dog jumped at him, grabbed his wrist and crunched down on it. At the same time the first dog jumped up and pushed David. He fell backwards onto the floor, the gun flying out of his hand. Without realizing what he was doing, David hollered, "Stop it, damn dog!"

Brick and Sally were awakened by the commotion. Lights came on from under the doors of the bedrooms. Brick quickly opened the door with his .357 in his hand and turned on the hall light as David was trying to reach for his gun. "Stop, whoever you are! Don't move!" Seeing Brick, the dogs let go of David and went down the hall a little; however they were still keeping a close eye on him, barking and growling fiercely. Brick hollered at them, "Red! Charlie! Hush!"

Sally carefully opened her door. "What's going .....?" She never finished her question. When she recognized who was out there she gasped, "Oh my God...David!" She grabbed her chest and stepped back into the doorway of her room hoping to be half sheltered.

David snarled at Sally, "Yeah, ya damn whore. I knew I could get you." In a rage, David quickly rolled over reaching for the revolver. Sally screamed. The dogs barked as Brick fired three shots killing David instantly.

Blood was oozing from David's chest. "Is he dead?" She was shaking and crying as she ran to Brick's side.

"Hang on, I'll check." Brick kicked the revolver away from David's hand then knelt down to check his pulse. "Yes, he's dead. Go get my phone. I have to make some calls." Sally ran into his bedroom to get the phone. Panting heavily, Red and Charlie came up to Brick. "It's ok, boys," he said as he petted their heads. "It's ok."

Sally ran to Brick and gave him the phone. Her hand was shaking so badly she almost dropped it when she handed it to him. "Oh my God, Brick, what's going to happen?"

Brick dialed the phone, and put his arm around Sally as the phone was ringing. "Everything is going to be ok, Sally. He's not going to bother you anymore."

A voice came on the phone, "Sheriff's office. How may I help you?"

"Bonnie. This is Sheriff Walls. I need you to send a deputy, an ambulance, and a coroner to my house immediately. I had to shoot an armed burglar."

"Yes, Sir. They'll be right there." Bonnie hung up and immediately called the ambulance, as well as, Deputy Watkins.

Brick held Sally closer as she continued to whimper. "I'm sorry you had to see that, Sally. He left me no choice when he rolled over to get that gun. I wasn't going to stand by and watch you get hurt." He kissed her on the top of the head. "Let's get some clothes on. They'll be here soon."

As soon as Brick was dressed, he took the dogs out into the backyard. As he walked toward the side yard, he noticed the gate was open.

"Damn it! I never thought about locking that gate. So that's how he got into the back yard, but I could have sworn that I locked the back door." He could hear the emergency vehicles coming down the street. "What am I going to do with the dogs? I can't touch the gate, 'cause that's how David came in, and the investigator will want to finger print it. Hell, I guess I'll take them in, and see if they'll stay in the living room." He called to the dogs just as the emergency vehicles came to a stop in front of the house.

CHAPTER TWENTY

When Brick walked back into the house, he asked Sally to put a leash on each dog and sit with them in the living room to keep them away from the crime scene, and then he opened the front door.

Deputy Albert Watkins was the first to walk in. "Are you ok, Sheriff?" He asked as he started looking around the room.

"Yeah, Albert, I'm ok."

"I called in the state troopers, too. I figured they would need to take over the investigation since you're the sheriff and it happened at your house."

"Thanks, Albert. Good thinking."

By this time, the entire neighborhood, had been aroused and came out to see what was going on at Brick's place. Several had wandered over to Brick's front yard, which made it difficult for the paramedics to get the gurney to the house and up the stairs to the door.

Brick took the men down the hall to the crime scene. As the paramedics checked the body, Albert started asking Brick some questions.

"So, what happened here? Why is Sally here? Is she tied up in all of this, too?"

"Hold on, Albert. Before you go too far remember the guy, David, I had Billy Roy check on?" Albert nodded his head. "Well, that's him."

"Oh, ok, I understand now. That's why you had Sally stay here with you because you wanted to protect her if this guy showed up."

"Right. Now let's wait for the troopers to get here before we go any farther."

"Yes, Sir. Is Sally ok?"

"Yeah, she's shaken up, but she'll be ok." One of the paramedics stood up to talk with Brick.

"Sheriff, it looks like a bullet went straight through his heart. He probably died instantly. We'll have to wait for the coroner to do his investigation and pronounce him dead before he can be moved." The other paramedic stood up and they all walked toward the living room.

Sally was doing her best to keep the dogs settled down by petting and talking to them. Even though they were behaving, the dogs still kept their eyes on the unfamiliar faces of the people walking in the house. Neither of them liked strangers in the house to start with, and after what had gone on tonight, they were really being protective of their home. Once in a while they'd give a low growl just to let the strangers know they were still there.

About ten minutes after the paramedics arrived, the state troopers pulled up in front of the house. Because this was Brick's residence, and because he had been involved in the shooting, they knew they would be in charge of the investigation. As they got out of the car, the troopers encouraged the neighbors to go back to their homes. Some asked questions of the troopers who shook their heads 'no' as they walked up the front steps and into the house.

Brick greeted them with a hand shake. "I'm Sheriff Brick Walls, this is my deputy Albert Watkins, and the paramedics."

After exchanges were made, one of the troopers started asking questions while the other secured the crime scene.

"So, Sheriff, tell me what happened." The trooper was looking at Brick straight in the eyes waiting for a response.

"Apparently, this guy came through the side fence and into the back door. He was carrying a revolver. When the dogs started attacking him, he lost his footing and fell knocking the revolver out of his hand. I came out of the bedroom with my .357 pointed at him and called off the dogs. Miss Sally came out of the spare bedroom at about the same time. The guy told her he was going to kill her. He rolled over grabbing the revolver, so I shot him. That's about it."

The trooper asked, "Any idea who he is?" He was still looking directly at Brick.

Brick responded honestly, "Yeah, he's Sally's ex-husband, David Cosgrove."

The trooper seemed a little surprised that Brick knew the suspect. "I see. So you know him?"

"Yeah, we used to shoot pool together when we were teenagers." While I was away in the Army, he and Sally got married. After a while, he began to abuse her and ended up in prison after their divorce. He was just released a few weeks ago, and called her earlier today, threatening to kill her, so I had her stay with me until we got him located. He apparently entered the house through the back gate and door and the dogs woke us up barking at him." As Brick answered the question, the coroner came walking through the front door.

"I assume the body is in here." The other trooper guarding the crime scene heard him and motioned him into the hall.

After checking over the body thoroughly, the coroner came in the living room and walked up to Brick and the trooper. "He's definitely dead." He turned to the trooper, "Are your crime scene technicians on the way out?"

"Yes, they were dispatched at the same time we were." He saw a flashing light in the front street through the open front door. "In fact, I think that's them now." The technicians began their job of taking pictures, dusting for fingerprints, and checking for other evidence that might have a bearing on the incident.

When they finished investigating outside, Sally asked if she could let the dogs out in the back yard. It had been almost three hours, and the dogs were ready for a break. Brick walked outside to lock the gate then let the dogs out.

The crime scene technicians were ready to leave about forty minutes later. The coroner accompanied the body to his office, and the state troopers left to file their reports. Deputy Watkins said as he was leaving, "Sheriff, I cleaned up the blood so that you wouldn't have to deal with it. See you at the office."

Brick replied, "Thank you so much, Albert. Good night." He locked the front door and turned off the porch light then turned and looked at Sally. "Are you gonna be ok, Sally?"

She looked down at the two dogs that came in a few minutes before. "Yes, I'm going to be fine." She bent over to rub the dogs' heads. "Thanks to these two wonderful dogs, and to you, Brick." She looked into Brick's eyes.

"They're pretty good watch dogs. Who would have known?" He reached down to pet the dogs, too. He looked at Sally and said, "At least you don't have to worry about David's threats anymore."

"I know. Thank, God. Now I can go back to my job and my home and everything is going to be alright."

"Yes, it is." He walked over to her. "I don't think I can go back to sleep right now. Would you like to sit out on the back porch and have some coffee with me?"

Sally looked at Brick and said, "Of course, I'd love to." Brick started the coffee while Sally got the cups. Red and Charlie were wagging their tails in anticipation of getting a treat.

"Here boys," Brick said as he gave both of the dogs a special treat. "Let's go back outside for a few minutes." He opened the door and both dogs ran outside, holding their treats in their mouths.

Sally poured the coffee into the cups and gave one to Brick as they both walked onto the porch. The Texas sun was starting to show itself on the horizon while the stars in the sky continued to twinkle. "What a beautiful sunrise," Sally commented as they sipped their coffee.

CHAPTER TWENTY-ONE

Brick woke up and looked at the clock on the nightstand. It was nine o'clock. As tired as he was from all that had happened just hours before, he knew he had to get up and go into work. He started the shower hoping that it wouldn't wake Sally. They stayed on the porch earlier that morning for only an hour, but Brick was glad they had. Most of the time was spent quietly.... sipping their coffee, watching the sun come up and enjoying the birds stopping by Mom's Garden looking for any bugs they could snack on. It was a healing they both needed.

He finished his shower, got dressed, and let the dogs outside. There were a couple of doughnuts left in the sack on the kitchen bench that he ate while the dogs were running. When he finished his quick breakfast, he quietly called the dogs back into the house. Sally was obviously still asleep, so he left the house and headed for his truck. He noticed that David's car was still parked in front of his house. "When I get to work, I'll have to call a tow truck to come and take the car to the impound lot," he said to himself as he climbed in his truck and drove to work.

When he walked into the building, Juanita and Billy Roy were standing in the front office drinking coffee and talking. They quickly put their cups down and went up to Brick.

"Are you ok? What happened?" Juanita asked. It was obvious she was very concerned about Brick.

"Yeah, I'm ok...just a little tired. Didn't get much sleep."

Billy Roy said, "Albert filled me in on the details when we changed shifts. I'm so glad you got that jerk before he got you or Miss Sally."

"Yeah, me, too! Well, I need to get some paperwork done. I'll be in my office with the door closed. Let me know if you need me." Brick dragged into his office shutting the door behind him. "It's gonna be tough trying to stay awake today, but I have to get the details of last night down on paper before I forget something that just might save my ass later on." He sat down in his chair, turned on his computer and began the arduous task of recording everything that happened.

It was about noon when Juanita knocked on Brick's office door. "What is it?"

"Sheriff, I am sorry to bother you, but Miss Sally is on the line and wants to speak to you."

Hearing Sally's name pulled him out of the funk he was in. "Yeah, put her through."

Juanita left and transferred the call. "Brick, it's Sally."

"Hi, Sally, are you ok?" It was good to hear her voice. She sounded as if she got a few hours of sleep.

"Yes, I'm doing fine, but I need to talk with you about something."

"Ok, what is it?" He was curious what she had on her mind.

"Brick, I need to move back to my house. I have to get some things done before I go back to work tomorrow. I certainly appreciate you're taking me in, but now is the time for me to get back on my feet and rebuild my life."

"I understand, Sally."

"But we can still get together again. How about this evening at six o'clock?"

"Getting together again sounds great to me. I'm not so keen about you leaving, but you have to do what you have to do."

Sally was so glad Brick understood her position. "I do. Thanks so much Brick. We'll talk later, ok?"

"Of course, Sally. I'll see you this evening. Be careful. Bye." Sally said good bye and hung up the phone.

Brick was busy the rest of the day with visits from the mayor, two city councilmen, and finally the investigator for the state troopers. The mayor and a couple of county commissioners just wanted to make sure he was alright and express their concerns about any liability the city or county might have. After Brick gave them his story, it seemed to settle them down a little bit, but they were still a little uneasy about the whole incident.

The meeting with the investigator was quite different from the meetings with the city and county representatives. The questions the investigator asked were preliminary in nature. Brick could tell during the conversation that the state trooper wasn't totally sure that it was a righteous shooting. The investigator told Brick he would get back with him with more questions. This whole situation weighted heavily on Brick's mind as he shut down his computer and got ready to go home.

Red was eagerly waiting for Brick. He barked multiple times when he heard Brick drive up to the house. Brick was thankful that neither Red, nor Charlie got hurt during the shooting that morning. As Brick opened the door, Red ran to him and jumped up putting his front paws on Brick's chest nearly knocking him over. "Whoa Boy, get down. Everything's ok." Red wanted lots of attention and petting from Brick. After a few minutes, Brick walked him out onto the porch in the back yard. He walked over to get the hose and then he watered Mom's Garden. The flowers were hardy, as were the herbs his mom had planted years ago. Brick was so glad that he had continued to keep up the garden for his mom. It meant more to him than he ever thought it would.

When he finished the watering, he went in to fix Red his dinner then went to his room to get ready to go to Sally's. Walking through the hall gave him a creepy feeling. To think that just hours before, he had shot and killed a man in that very area. Brick realized it was going to take some time to get past this. He went into his room to change his clothes then let Red out again for a few minutes before leaving for Sally's.

When he arrived at Sally's she already had the food on the table. "Sally, this food smells delicious. You are quite a cook." He took the glass of wine she poured for him and sat down.

"Thank you, Brick. I'm so glad you like my cooking. I've always loved to cook, and it's nice having someone around to appreciate it." She smiled as Brick lifted his glass. "To the best cook ever!" Sally laughed as they clinked their glasses together.

After they finished their meal, Brick filled their glasses again, and they went into the living room to talk. "Brick, how can I ever repay you for the kindness you have shown me? I probably shouldn't say this, but Brick I think I'm falling in love with you. I'm sorry, but that's how I feel." She looked down, feeling a little embarrassed.

Brick was almost speechless. He had wanted their relationship to grow to the next level, and now that she expressed her feelings, he knew he could share his feelings with her. "Sally, please don't apologize for telling me how you feel. To tell you the truth, I hate leaving you at the end of the evening. I want to spend all the time I can with you. You see, I'm falling in love with you, too." He put his glass on the table, put his arms around Sally, and gave her a passionate kiss. As she pushed up against him, Brick could feel the heat from her body, and he was sure she could feel the arousal in him.

As their lips parted, Brick whispered, "I want to make love to you, Sally."

Sally starred into Brick's blue eyes and responded, "I want to make love with you, too, Brick." She stood up and reached out her hand never taking her eyes off of his. Brick took her hand in his and she led him to her bedroom.

They took off each other's clothes, only pausing to caress and kiss. He laid her gently on the bed and said, "I believe this is going to be a wonderful lifelong relationship."

CHAPTER TWENTY-TWO

The next morning, Sally went to the restaurant and told her best friend, Amanda Johnson, who was the restaurant manager, the good news about her renewed relationship with Brick. They hugged each other.

"Oh that's so great, Sally. How wonderful! I know that all your life you've wanted that man."

"I love him so much, Amanda. I guess I always have, and now it looks like we may be together forever." Sally's smile and sparkling eyes seemed to brighten up the entire room as the two friends got busy serving their hungry customers.

Meanwhile, Brick was working in his office when a call came in about a disturbance down at the pool hall. Two men were about to get into a fistfight. Because the deputies were still out on other calls, Brick had to answer this call himself.

"Juanita, I'll be down at the pool hall. As soon as a deputy clears from a call, send him down to help me."

"Yes, sir, be careful." Brick was already out the door and on his way to his car.

When he arrived, he observed an argument between two large men who were shouting and pushing each other obviously ready to get into a fight. Brick walked up to them, "Alright, that's enough of this. Stop right now!"

One man turned to him and said, "You keep out of this, Sheriff, this is between us."

Brick stepped forward, "There will be no fighting going on in here." With that, the man turned and hit Brick hard in the chest knocking him backwards. Brick locked eyes with the man as he stepped forward. "You're under arrest! Turn around and put your hands behind you." As Brick reached for his handcuffs, the man took another swing at him almost connecting with Brick's chin. That was all Brick needed. He punched the man hard in the face and attempted to turn him around so that he could get him handcuffed.

Meanwhile, the second man and the rest of the men in the pool hall stepped back from the fight just in time to see Brick being taken down. The big man grabbed Brick and pulled him down to the floor. Brick wrestled around with him for several minutes until he was finally on top.

"Have you had enough? Are you gonna stop?" Brick shouted, but the man started trying to hit him again, so Brick punched him in the face a second time. That seemed to daze the man, which gave Brick time to get off of him and roll him over. He cuffed the man's hands behind his back. "Come on," he said as he roughly stood the man up, "You're going to jail." He turned his head and looked at the first man. "What about you?"

"I never wanted to fight. It was his fault. He started it." It was evident that the man was shaken up a bit.

"Alright." Brick said as he walked the prisoner to the door. "I want you to come down now and give me a statement regarding how this whole thing started. Understand?" Brick looked him square in the eye so there would be no room for doubt.

"Yes, sir Sheriff. I'll be right there."

When Brick led the prisoner out of the door and to the squad car, the noise in the pool hall picked up as the customers talked about the fight and then resumed their activities.

As they arrived at the sheriff's office, Brick parked the car, opened the door, pulled the man out, and walked him up to the door.

"Sheriff, it was all Dan's fault, honestly."

"Yeah, right," Brick said as he walked him into the building. "It wasn't Dan's fault that you decided to turn a misdemeanor into a felony and assault a law enforcement officer while you were resisting arrest, was it? Juanita, I need the keys to cell one right now."

"Yes, sir." Juanita retrieved the keys immediately and gave them to Brick. Deputy Watkins walked into the building about that time, saw what was going on and offered to take the man to the jail cell.

The phone started ringing. Brick said, "I'll handle him. You're probably needed to answer that call anyway."

He could hear Juanita saying to the person on the phone, "Yes, ma'am. I'll send a deputy out right now." Deputy Watkins picked up the paper with the information Juanita had written and after making sure that Brick had his prisoner safely locked behind bars, immediately left.

Brick opened the cell. He took the handcuffs off the man, shoved him in the cell, and slammed the cell door shut. "You're gonna sit there for a while and cool off, then I'll get you booked in." As he left the cell block, the other fighter entered the building. "Is your name, Dan?" Brick asked.

"Yes, sir." Dan's eyes were very wide open. He still was not sure that he was going to keep from getting charged with something for his part in the argument.

"What is your last name, Dan?"

"It's Gregory, sir, Dan Gregory. Am I in trouble here?"

"Come in my office, Dan, and tell me what happened."

They both entered Brick's office so that Brick could take his statement and complete the paperwork on the incident. "First off, did you know the man you were fighting with?"

"Yes, I do Sheriff. His name is Arny Wilcoxson. He and I shoot pool here every once in a while, or at least we used to. I don't know what got into him today. We were drinking beer and shooting, and I was winning. It seemed to irritate him for some reason. Then I accidentally bumped his arm as he was trying to line up a shot, and he just lost it completely. He started cussing me and wouldn't stop, so I cussed him back, and then he pushed me. Well, I wasn't going to take that from the son-of-a-bitch, so I pushed him back and I guess that's about the time that you walked in and stopped us."

Dan continued after taking a deep breath. "I'm really sorry for all the fuss. I never wanted to fight him. He's bigger than I am to start with, and besides that, I didn't want to get into no trouble with the law. My old lady would kick my ass up between my shoulder blades if I went and got myself arrested for fighting. And I damned sure didn't want no part of him hittin' you like he did. It ain't right to hit a police officer. You can get into a WHOLE lot of trouble for doing something like that! That's just stupid! I really don't want to go to jail over this, Sheriff. Are we finished now? Can I please go on home?"

Brick sized him up and decided he was telling the truth. "Yeah, I guess I've got everything that I need from you. Listen Dan, you know that I could lock you up too, for getting into the shoving match with Wilcoxson. That's disorderly conduct in a public place. But because you stopped when I told you to, I'm going to cut you some slack this time." Brick got up from his desk and looked squarely into Dan's eyes. "Just make sure that you don't get into another incident like this again, because the next time I will lock you up for sure." Dan nodded his head in agreement. And I'd better not find out that you started the argument or you will see me again, and you won't like the results. Do we understand each other on that?"

"Oh yes, sir, Sheriff. You won't get any trouble out of me, I'll guarantee you. This is as close as I ever want to get to goin' to jail."

Brick walked Dan Gregory out to the lobby, then went back into the jail area to finish booking in Arny Wilcoxson. He had cooled off somewhat and became more cooperative, so Brick let him have his phone call when he finished getting the information for the arrest paperwork. Wilcoxson called a family member to get them to hire an attorney for him. After he had returned the prisoner to his cell, Brick went back to his office and finished his reports.

Later that afternoon, Brick met Sally at the restaurant for coffee and a piece of pie. Sally saw the bruises on Brick's face and hands as he sat down at the table. "Oh my gosh, Brick, what happened to you?"

"I answered a call about a fight at the pool hall. Unfortunately, one of the guys decided to fight me, too. Needless to say, he's cooling off in a jail cell right now." Sally shook her head as she got up to get their order.

As he waited for Sally to come back, he noticed a stranger sitting at another table. When Sally came back with the food and drinks, Brick looked at the gentleman and asked, "Sally, do you know that man?"

"What man?" she replied. Brick motioned to the table across the room.

Sally turned to look at the man who was quietly eating his lunch. "No, but he looks like he's from South America or Central Mexico. I wonder what he is doing in Maranda?"

Brick thought about going over to introduce himself to the stranger, but when the man saw Brick looking at him, he quickly threw some money on the table and left. Brick had a curious look on his face. "Is there something wrong?" Sally asked.

"No, just wondering why he seemed quick to leave when we looked over at him. Oh well, let's finish up. I have to get back and finish the paperwork on the pool hall incident."

As he got into his rented car which was parked in front of the restaurant, Roberto said to himself, "Now I know who Brick Walls is and what he looks like. I must telephone the boss and let him know that I have already located him. Carlos didn't say anything about him being the sheriff, though. Not that it makes any difference. When you piss off the boss, you die. At least he will be easy to relocate when the time comes to kill him. I wonder if this new sheriff has the dope and the money that disappeared. Carlos would be very happy with me if I could recover those and kill this asshole, too. I would really be his number one hombre if I could do that."

CHAPTER TWENTY-THREE

It appeared that things had started to settle down that afternoon after Brick arrived back from coffee with Sally. There weren't very many calls that morning, and it looked like it was going to be a quiet rest of the afternoon. Both deputies checked in with very little to report…two tickets for speeding and one for littering the highway.

Bonnie was working at her desk when the phone rang. "Sheriff's office. Can I help you?"

The voice of a very agitated young woman responded, "Yes. I need the Sheriff…please send him out, now!"

"I need to know who's calling and what is the problem?" She picked up her pencil ready to take down the facts.

"This is Georgia Fisher. I live out on route 376…#12 on route 376. There's a man trying to break into my house. He's pounding the door right now. He came to the door earlier and made a grab at me, so I slammed the door on him. Now he's trying to break the door down. Please send the sheriff out now!"

Bonnie took down the information. "Yes, ma'am. Please calm down. Put something up against the door to keep him out, and we'll be there as soon as we can. Find a place to hide in…a closet or some place until we can get there." Bonnie was walking into Brick's office with the information as she talked to the woman.

"Please hurry...hurry," the woman screamed as she hung up.

Brick immediately had Bonnie call Billy Roy and George to meet him at the scene. He went to his car and quickly headed for route 376.

While Brick and the deputies were hurrying to the scene, the man managed to break into the house and found Georgia hiding in the front closet. He grabbed her and pulled her into the bedroom. He threw her on the bed and started pulling her clothes off. She was fighting and screaming, but she couldn't do much against the powerful grip he had on her. "Stop..stop, please," she pleaded.

The man closed his grip even tighter. "You stop fighting me, and I won't hurt you. If you don't stop fighting me, I'll have to kill you."

As soon as he saw the house Brick pulled up and got out of the car with his revolver in his hand. The front door of the old wooden house had been kicked in and was standing open. The deputies arrived a few seconds after Brick. They came out of their cars with their shotguns pointed at the house. Brick told Billy Roy to go around to the back and keep the intruder from leaving. George was given orders to stay and watch the front of the house. Brick cautiously entered the house through the broken front door.

In the bedroom, the man finished pulling Georgia's clothes off. He was about to unfasten his own pants when he heard a voice. It was Brick. "Ma'am...Ma'am are you all right?"

"HELP! HELP!" Brick heard the woman scream from the room down the hall from where he was standing. He quickly pulled his radio out of his pocket and told the deputies the man was there and to enter the house carefully. With his revolver pointed at the hall where the noise was coming from, Brick carefully started to enter the hall. The deputies had hurried in and were now right behind him.

"Don't come any closer. If you come into this room, I'll kill her," the man threatened.

Brick hollered back, "Now don't do anything crazy. So far you haven't killed or hurt anyone, and that's the way I want this to end. It won't do you any good to kill her, because you'll be up for life or be executed. Don't do anything foolish."

"Don't come in here. Just leave and I'll go away."

"I can't do that. It doesn't work that way."

"Just don't come in here. Go away. I'm gonna listen for you to leave, or I'm going to kill her." Georgia was whimpering and kept whispering for someone to help her.

Brick turned to the deputies and gave them hand signals to stand by outside, while he spoke so that the man would hear him, "Alright men, let's do as he says and leave." The deputies made some noise as they left, hoping to trick the man to believing they did. In the meantime, Brick positioned himself flat against the wall behind the bedroom door.

Everything got real quiet except for the whimpering of Georgia. The man listened very carefully for any sign of someone in the house, but it sounded like no one was there. He turned to Georgia and said, "Alright Lady, now you just be quiet." He took a piece of her clothing and tied it around her mouth to keep her from screaming. Then he took another piece and tied her hands behind her. "I'm gittin' out of here, and don't you tell anybody, or I'll come looking for you. Do you understand?" He looked straight into her eyes. Georgia nodded her head in fear.

He carefully went to the doorway and started down the hall when Brick came out from behind the door and hit him on his head with the revolver temporarily knocking the man to the floor unconscious.

Not knowing the outcome of the confrontation, Georgia started crying and tried to holler for help. It was when she heard Brick's voice that she knew she had been saved.

"Everything's ok, ma'am. Everything's ok." Brick radioed the deputies to come in then went to check on Georgia. He entered the bedroom as Georgia was trying to get her hands loose.

Although she was naked, Brick kept his eyes away from her while he untied her hands. "I'm going to step out while you get dressed. Then I'll need to take a statement from you." He walked out of the room shutting the door behind him giving Georgia the respect she deserved.

The man was starting to gain consciousness just as the deputies entered the house. "Ah-h-h my head," the man said as the deputies rolled him over and put handcuffs on him.

"Come on, we're taking you to jail," Billy Roy said as the deputies pulled the man up to his feet.

Brick came out of the bedroom and walked over to the man, "You're lucky it's just your head that hurts. I could have shot you and probably should have. This country would be better off with you out of here." The deputies took him to Billy Roy's squad car, strapped him in and then headed for the jail.

Georgia finished dressing and came out to talk to Brick. It was obvious she was very embarrassed since he had seen her without clothes. Knowing how she must feel, Brick kept the conversation short and to the point. "Are you all right?"

Georgia shook her head, "Yes, sir. Thank you so much for helping me....I don't know...," she started to cry.

"It's ok. You're going to be fine, Georgia. It is Georgia, right?" She shook her head yes.

"We want you to file charges on this man."

"Oh, I will. I will," she said emphatically. "My husband's out of town this week, and I don't know what to do."

"Do you have any other family close by?"

"Yes, my mother and father live twenty-four miles from here."

"Do you need any help to..." She cut him off.

"No, I can do it."

"I suggest you call them and make plans to spend the rest of the week with them. Will you be leaving tonight?" She shook her head no. "Are you going to be ok tonight?"

"Yes, I have a friend I can spend the night with."

"Ok, but stop by the office tomorrow before you go, so we can get the paperwork done." She nodded her head "yes". Brick stood up and walked to the broken door. "I'll call a buddy of mine who can fix this door, so you can lock it up tonight."

"Thank you so much!"

Brick dialed his friend's phone number and made arrangements for him to come over. "Great! Thanks, Bill." He hung up the phone. "Bill is on his way. Would you like me to wait on the porch until he arrives?"

"Please....I just don't think I can trust anyone right now."

"Go ahead and make your calls. I'll be here until Bill gets the job done." With that being said, Georgia went for her phone, as Brick walked out on the porch and called the office. "Juanita, is everything ok there?"

"Yes, sir. The deputies brought the man in and booked him. He sure was complaining about his head hurting."

"Have the ambulance driver come over and check him out. He'll probably just give the man an aspirin. Oh, by the way, what is this guy's name?"

"Let me look at the paper. He's Harold Atkins."

"Harold Atkins," Brick repeated. "Well it looks like Mr. Harold Atkins is going to be the guest of the state for quite a while." He told Juanita he would be at the victim's home until Bill finished fixing the door and to call him if he was needed. They hung up and Brick sat down on the porch chair to wait for Bill. He smiled to himself. "I just thought it was a quiet day."

CHAPTER TWENTY-FOUR

The next day a call came into the sheriff's office regarding a stranger walking around on the property next to Brick's where the plane had crashed and burned almost a year and a half ago. It was the same field where Brick and Red had inadvertently gotten involved in a drug deal gone bad, which resulted in several deaths, and also resulted in him being stalked by a crooked sheriff, his predecessor, which is why he ended up living in Las Vegas for almost a half of a year.

Juanita dispatched a deputy to the field to investigate, but by the time he arrived, there was no one around. When Brick got back to the office, Juanita told him about the sighting. Brick was a little more than curious about who would be out there and what would be the reason, but he had too much paperwork to get completed so he turned his attention to his work. He made a mental note to go out to the field later that day or the next to see if he noticed anything different out there. Brick had a bad feeling about it and hoped that he wasn't becoming paranoid about the field and its subsequent bad memories.

Later that morning a call came in regarding an abandoned car on county road 271. Juanita dispatched a deputy to check out the car in case it had been stolen. She wondered if it had anything to do with the man who had been seen wandering in the field next to Brick's earlier. However, it turned out to be a mechanical problem and by the time the deputy located the car, there was already someone there to tow it to a repair shop.

⚜

Roberto drove his rented car to the Phillips 66 convenience store and gas station in town. After he filled up, he went into the store. "Do you have a coke?" He asked the attendant.

"Yeah, right back there." The attendant pointed to the glass-door coolers that lined the back of the store.

"Would you like a coke?" Roberto asked as he walked back to get his own drink.

"Naw, I don't believe so, thank ya."

Roberto got a drink from the cooler along with a bag of chips and came back to the attendant at the cash register. "Anything go on around this town?" He asked as he paid the attendant and opened his drink.

The attendant replied with a slight chuckle. "Well, not much has happened around here since we elected our new sheriff, but quite a bit went on a while back." Roberto listened intently as the attendant proceeded to tell his customer all about the plane crash and the story about the money and the chase out to Las Vegas by the crooked former sheriff.

"Ah, so somebody's got the money, huh?" Roberto was listening intently to the answer.

"Naw, naw. It got blown up along with the old sheriff according to the authorities. Nobody got any money and nobody got any drugs. Just a bunch of killings. Kind of a dumb thing if you ask me."

Roberto looked disappointed. "Yeah, yeah, sure. Well, thank you very much. Adios." Roberto left the gas station and went back to his motel room. He needed to report this right away and pulled out his cell phone then dialed the number for Carlos. Carlos was not going to like this news and Roberto was more than a little nervous about making the call.

After two rings, Carlos answered, "Si,"

"Carlos, this is Roberto. I have news for you."

Carlos was all ears as he listened to the results of Roberto's findings. His anticipation subsided and turned to anger as he heard Roberto explain about the plane crash and the lost money and drugs. "I don't get nothing back? What kind of crap is that?"

Roberto replied, "That's what it looks like."

Carlos quickly turned his focus on Brick. "Did you find out about this Brick Walls?"

"Si, I found him, but I don't think he got anything out of it. It turns out he went and got himself elected sheriff around here after our former friend got himself blown up trying to recapture the money."

Carlos was becoming furious, "He's the one who caused all the problems. I don't give a damn if he got himself elected governor of the state. Kill him as quickly as you can and then get your ass back here."

Roberto had heard that tone of voice from Carlos before, and he knew that if he didn't kill Brick, Carlos would make sure that his life would be cut short. "Si, Carlos. Adios." As he put his phone down, Roberto had already started working on a plan to carry out Carlos's order.

After a long day at the office, Brick was leaving at six thirty that evening when he thought about Sally and decided to see if she would like to meet him for dinner. He got in his truck and dialed her number.

"Hello?"

He loved hearing her voice. "Hi, Sally. It's me, Brick. Would you like to have dinner with me this evening?"

"Oh, how sweet, Brick. I'd love to, but I just finished pulling dinner out of the oven. Why don't you come over and have dinner here."

"What are we having?" Brick said sheepishly.

Sally laughed, "Does it really matter?"

"I'll be there after I take care of Red. Ok?"

"Of course, I'll put it back in the oven to keep warm." She was smiling as they hung up. "I hope that someday I will be his wife and fix him dinner every night in our home," she said as she put another place setting on the table.

Meanwhile, Brick hurried home to let Red out and feed him. "Hey, big dog," he said as Red met him at the door with his tail wagging with excitement. He petted Red's big hairy head then let him out in the back yard. The dog ran all over the back yard at full speed and then began to search for a spot to relieve himself.

The moon was slowly climbing in the sky as the sun sank below the horizon. Brick stepped out on the porch to enjoy the sight. He thought about the several times he and Sally had watched a Texas sunset together. There was simply nothing so majestic as a Texas sunset, especially when there were clouds in the sky that reflected the rays of the setting sun in many different colors.

He also thought about the night when she led him to her bedroom. Brick knew he wanted Sally to be a part of his life forever and he was also certain that she wanted the same thing. He knew it was time to take the next step and formalize their relationship. He called Red inside and fed him then quickly headed to Sally's house.

Sally and Brick talked about their day as they enjoyed the cheese and jalapeno enchiladas that she prepared. "Sally, you are such an excellent cook! Everything you make is superb....even the green glop you made." They both chuckled at the memory.

After they finished dinner, they went into the living room to sit on the couch. Nothing had been mentioned yet about the previous evening, and Sally wasn't sure what Brick had on his mind at this moment.

Brick took her hand and looked into Sally's eyes. He knew this was the right time. "Sally, I love you. Will you marry me?"

Sally took a slight gasp, "Oh, Brick. I love you, too. Of course I'll marry you." They held each other intensely as they kissed passionately. When they broke to catch their breath, Sally said, "Brick, you have made my dream come true." Brick didn't speak, but pulled her even closer and kissed her again. He finally felt at peace, and he knew this was going to last forever.

CHAPTER TWENTY-FIVE

Roberto decided to go to the Sweet Pea Café to make some more observations and to come up with a plan to get rid of Brick. He considered several options including following him home and killing him there. "I've got to figure out a way to get this done quickly and get out of town so they won't suspect me," he thought to himself as he finished his coffee. "I can go to the sheriff's office and shoot him. There doesn't seem to be much traffic around the building. I could get away before they even know what happened. Maybe tomorrow. Yeah, tomorrow." He smiled as he paid the tab and left the building.

❈

The next morning Roberto parked a little ways from the sheriff's office, but close enough where he could see who came and went. Brick showed up at eight o'clock, unaware that Roberto was parked across the street watching him. Roberto smiled and thought, "Sheriff Walls, you will have to leave for lunch sometime, and when you do, I'll have something waiting for you."

❈

Earlier that morning, Deputy George Kimbell rolled over and turned off his alarm clock. "Dang, it's already seven-thirty. I've got to get up and get some things done before I check in to work at noon." He rolled back over and patted Gloria on her buttocks. "Honey, honey, it's time to get up."

She opened her eyes slowly, "Are you sure?"

"Yeah, come on." He leaned over to kiss her then got out of bed.

"Ok, I'll fix breakfast," she said as she rolled over to the edge of the bed and got up. "I was sleeping so good. George Kimbell you're going to owe me." They both laughed and started their daily routine. "Isn't this so much better than when we were in Battle Creek, Michigan? You were working out there in the cold and wet and terrible conditions in the winter time, and I was always worried about you having an accident, or getting hurt on the job."

George walked over to Gloria and gave her a kiss. "Yes, I'm so glad we decided to chuck the job in Michigan and come to Texas. I was so fortunate there was an opening here at the sheriff's department, and I was able to immediately get back to work. I'm very happy we made that decision!"

"I am, too, George!" She said as she gazed into his eyes and smiled.

He gave her a big hug then said, "I'm hungry. Let's eat." They laughed as they walked to the kitchen.

It was after eleven o'clock when George started getting ready for work. He was just putting on his gun belt when Gloria came in the room. "Honey, please be careful at work today."

He reached over and gave her a kiss and hug. "I always am. Don't worry about me. I'll be alright."

"I know, but just be extra careful today, please?"

He could tell she was a little nervous. "What's wrong, Honey?"

"It's just a funny little feeling I have. I'm sure it's nothing, but I just want you to be safe."

He took her in his arms and kissed her again. "I promise I'll be extra careful today. Now I have to go. See ya later. Have a great day." They waved at each other as he left the house to get into the car.

George turned on the radio as he pulled out of the driveway. Classic country music was playing. He leaned back a little with a smile on his face. "Ah, this is the life! Nice weather and nice music. It doesn't get any better than this."

As he was coming up on the sheriff's department, he noticed a car parked across the street from the front door. "Huh, I wonder what's going on?" When he looked closer, he saw a hand coming out of the front window with a gun in it aimed at the front door of the sheriff's department. "Oh my God," he hollered as he rammed the front of his patrol car into the back of the car hoping to keep the man from shooting someone.

George jumped out of his car and drew his gun pointing it at Roberto. "Drop that gun right now," he ordered. Roberto had just jumped out of his car, turned facing George and fired a shot at him. George fell to the concrete.

"I've got to get the hell out of here," Roberto said as he jumped back in the car and took off.

Brick and his staff heard the car crash and then the shot. He told the ladies to stay inside while he went out to investigate. As he opened the door he saw George fall to the concrete and a black sedan speeding off. Brick drew his gun and looked around for anyone else that might have a gun drawn. He quickly made his way to George. "George, are you alright? What happened here?" Then Brick saw the blood oozing from George's shoulder.

George was moaning and holding his arm. "Yeah, that damn son-of-a-bitch! This guy was sitting in his car when I drove up behind him. I noticed he was pointing a gun at the front door of the building. I tried to stop him, but he shot me in the shoulder. I'm sorry Sheriff, I tried to get him."

"Yeah, well you don't worry about that. Let's get you some help." Brick took out his cell phone and dialed 911. "This is Sheriff

Brick Walls. We have an officer shot and need an ambulance out here across from the Sheriff's Department right away. Thanks." Brick then asked George about the specifics of the car and the gunman. George tried his best to give Brick something to go on. He told him the back end was smashed in and that he thought he remembered the license plate falling off the car. Brick walked over in front of George's car and found the plate. He picked up the plate and got back on his cell phone.

Brick was trying to direct traffic as he waited for someone to answer the phone. "Sheriff's Department, this is Bonnie. How may I help you?"

"Bonnie, I want an all points bulletin out for a late model, black Chevy two-door with the back end crushed in and no license plate. Be aware the driver is armed and dangerous. Also, have Billy Roy come down here as soon as he can make it."

"Yes, sir. Is it all clear outside?"

"Yes," he said. He hung up the phone just as the ambulance was making its way around the corner.

"Sheriff," George said as the ambulance came to a stop. "Would someone call Gloria, please?"

"Sure will, George. Don't worry about anything. You just get well." They put him onto the stretcher, rolled him to the vehicle, loaded him in and took off for the hospital with the lights and siren still on.

Billy Roy drove up just as the ambulance pulled away. He got out of the car and started directing traffic. "Sheriff, is George going to be ok?"

"Yeah, he got shot in the shoulder, but he'll mend. Take over here while I go in and file a report." Brick walked to the building and into his office. "Juanita, call a wrecker for George's car. We need to have it checked and have the front end fixed." "Oh, and here," he handed her the license plate, "see if you can find out who owns this car."

"Yes, Sir. Is George going to be ok?"

"Yes, he was shot in the shoulder, but he'll be ok. Oh, that reminds me...get me his home phone number so I can call his wife."

"Ok, Sheriff." Juanita looked up the number and brought it to Brick immediately.

"Thanks, Juanita." She just smiled and nodded her head.

Brick was not excited about calling Gloria, but he knew she would want to know about George right away. He picked up the phone and dialed the number. After a couple of rings, Gloria answered.

"Hello." She sounded so happy, Brick really hated to change the mood.

"Gloria, this is Sheriff Walls. I'm calling to let you know there has been a little shoot out here...."

She interrupted, "Oh my God, is George all right?"

"Take it easy, Honey. Yes, he's all right, but he got shot in the shoulder."

Gloria was becoming hysterical by this point, "Oh God, where is he?"

"He's at the hospital, and I'll be right over to take you there."

"Oh, Sheriff, thank you. Thank you. I'll be ready." She hung up the phone before Brick had a chance to say good bye.

As he started out the door, Juanita said, "Sheriff, I've got a hit on this license plate."

"Great. Who does it belong to?"

"Well, it belongs to a car rental company located at the Houston airport."

Brick looked frustrated. "Oh crap. Alright, I'll check it out from there. Right now I'm going to the hospital. Let me know if you come up with anything new."

"I'll do it, Sheriff."

Brick drove to George's house and saw Gloria waiting for him in the driveway. She got in the car and immediately asked, "How is he? How is he?" She was trying hard to hold back the tears.

Brick tried to reassure her that George was going to be all right. "I don't think it's too serious. He did take a slug to the shoulder and that will have to be fixed, but he's going to be ok. The doctors are checking him out now, and they should have some more information on his status by the time we get to the hospital."

"Oh Lord, I was so afraid of this. Five years he's been in law enforcement and never got shot, and now he has."

"He's going to be ok, Gloria. He's going to be ok."

They arrived at the hospital and went into the emergency room area. Gloria ran up to the attendant at the admissions desk. "I'm Gloria Kindell. My husband was shot and...."

The attendant interrupted her. "Yes, ma'am, they have just taken him up to surgery to remove the bullet in his shoulder. Let me get the nurse for you." She left and came back with the nurse in charge of the emergency room.

"Hi, I'm Glenda. Your husband is in surgery to remove the bullet. It shouldn't last long. According to the x-rays, there doesn't appear to be any broken bones. He'll probably need to stay overnight though, so we can monitor his vital signs and make sure everything is all right."

"Oh thank God," Gloria said as she took a deep breath.

"Why don't you sit here in the waiting room, and I'll have Dr. Martinez come to talk with you as soon as your husband is out of surgery." Glenda continued, "Oh, would you like some water or coffee while you're waiting?"

Brick replied, "Yes, I think we both could use some coffee. Thank you, Glenda."

"Not a problem." She said as she left to go get the coffee.

Gloria sat down slowly, mesmerized by the whole incident. "Sheriff," she muttered as if in a trance. "I told him this morning I had this feeling that something was going to happen. I told him to be extra careful today. Who would have thought...." Her mind drifted away for a minute more. "Who would have thought..."

Glenda came in with the coffee which helped bring Gloria around. It wasn't too long before the doctor came in to speak with them. "Hi, I'm Dr. Martinez. Deputy Kimbell is doing fine. We removed the bullet and it looks like there was no other damage except for the tissue in his shoulder where the bullet passed through. He'll need to keep the dressing on for a few days. I'll see him next week. As soon as he feels up to it, he can go home. I see no reason to keep him. His vital signs are fine. He doesn't have any excess bleeding. I'd say he was a very lucky man." The doctor's smile was reassuring as he looked at Gloria.

"Oh, thank you so much doctor. Your nurse said he would probably have to stay overnight. Are you sure it's alright for him to come home?"

"Oh, yes. In fact, as he was coming out from the anesthesia he asked if he could leave now. I have a feeling he'll be coming through the door soon." They all chuckled.

Brick gave the doctor a handshake, "Thank you so much, Dr. Martinez."

"You're very welcome, Sheriff. I'm glad it wasn't worse."

Just then the door opened, and a nurse slowly wheeled George into the room. His shoulder was bandaged, and he had on a sling. Gloria hurried over and gave him a big hug and kiss.

"You didn't have to come to the hospital. It wasn't serious... just a scratch."

"Oh hush," Gloria said as she carefully hugged him again.

"Well, are you ready, George?"

"Yes, Sheriff, and thank you again, doctor." He shook the doctor's hand.

Glenda came out with the instructions on how to care for the wound. She gave them to the doctor, who gave them to Gloria. "Be sure he follows these instructions and call me immediately if he has any problems."

"Yes, Sir. Thank you again," she said as she followed Brick and George out the door.

As they were driving back to the Kimbell's home, Brick told George, "I want you to stay home and rest for a few days. After you see Dr. Martinez again, let me know when he thinks you can come back to work. We can put you on desk duty."

"But, Sheriff, I know you'll need me sooner than that."

"Naw, the other deputies can handle things, and if we have a major problem come up, I'll get the state troopers to help. Don't worry about it. You just take care of yourself." They drove into the driveway.

Brick helped George into the house. "And George, thank you for your bravery." George shook Brick's hand and Brick left.

CHAPTER TWENTY-SIX

Roberto reached Hwy 90 and pulled into the hotel where he was staying. He drove around to the back of the building so the car wouldn't be seen. He went in the back entrance and straight to his room, quickly packed up his things, and headed up the hall to the front desk.

The clerk at the desk noticed he had his bag with him, "Are you checking out, Sir?"

Roberto nodded his head as he stood there and looked around the room. As the clerk was getting his receipt she asked, "Well, did you get your business done?"

"No. Not quite. Is there a taxi or bus that runs from here to San Antonio?"

The clerk was a little surprised at the question. "Ah, no, Sir. That's a little far from here for a taxi, and buses don't stop here either. Don't you have your car?"

"Yeah, but I've got to turn it in to the rental place." Roberto was getting a little antsy with this entire conversation.

"Oh. Ok. Is there anything else I can do for you?"

"No," he said as he picked up his bag and walked out the front door. He stood on the sidewalk and put his bag down. "Damn, what in the hell am I going to do?" As he lit up a cigarette, he noticed a sports car pulling up into the driveway of the motel. He left his bag and walked a little closer to the front of the building.

The man got out of the car and asked Roberto, "Say, have they got any rooms available?"

"Yes, Sir. We sure do," Roberto responded cheerfully.

"Oh, do you work here?" The man asked as he started to remove his things from the car.

"Yes. I'm the parking attendant." Roberto couldn't believe the man was buying this.

"Great! Well I'll go in and get a room. Are you going to park my car?" Roberto nodded his head. The man was a little hesitant, but gave the keys to Roberto. "Thank you," He said as he gave Roberto a nice tip, then picked up his suitcases and strolled into the motel.

As soon as the man had walked into the building, Roberto grabbed his bag, threw it into the car, jumped in and took off for the highway. "I can't believe the sucker gave me a tip!" He laughed as he drove on to highway 90.

After giving it some thought he said, "Wait a minute. No one is going to recognize this car for a while, until the guy realizes it's missing. I need to go back to Maranda and finish the job I was sent here to do. That sheriff's not gonna know what hit him." He had a vicious laugh as he took an exit off the highway and made his way back on the road to Maranda.

CHAPTER TWENTY-SEVEN

Brick had just left George's house and was on his way back into town. He was thinking about the day's event, "I wonder where that bastard is? The best I can hope for is for someone to see the car and report it to the office." He was still going over the facts of the case, when he noticed he was coming upon Sally's restaurant. "I might as well stop for something to eat before I go back to the office."

The restaurant wasn't very busy when he walked in. Amanda was the manager and the waitress on duty at the time. "Hi, Sheriff," she said with a big smile. "Do you want a table?" Brick nodded "yes". Amanda remembered what Sally had shared with her about the first time she and Brick spent the night together. "Sally sure is a lucky gal," she thought as she led Brick to his table.

"Has Sally been in today?" Brick asked as he sat down.

"No, she hasn't been in yet. I think she's supposed to come in pretty soon."

"Ok. Well, I'll have a cup of coffee, if you don't mind." Brick decided to see if Sally showed up before he ordered any food.

"Yes, Sir," Amanda said as she walked back to the kitchen for Brick's coffee. Brick was trying to get his thoughts together, as a little sports car came up the street.

Roberto noticed the sheriff's car and smiled to himself. "Ah ha... I think I can finish my job now and then go home." He turned into the restaurant parking lot and pulled in almost next to Brick's car. He got out his weapon and checked it. "Now, I will get revenge. I take care of things for you, Carlos."

He walked into the restaurant, saw Brick seated at a table to his left. He turned toward Brick. "Ah ha...I want you to know this is the end for you."

Brick looked up and started to jump up. Just as Roberto fired, Amanda stepped in between them with Brick's coffee. "Ah," she dropped the coffee and screamed as the bullet went into her side. Brick pulled out his revolver, as Roberto fired again, this time hitting Brick in the side. Brick fired two shots. Both bullets struck Roberto...one in the head and one in the neck. Roberto's gun dropped out of his hand as he fell to the floor dead. Other customers in the restaurant were screaming just as Sally walked in the front door.

"Oh, my God! What's happening here?" Sally immediately saw Brick slumped over, blood dripping from his side. "Brick," she screamed as she ran to him. "Are you all right?" The tears were starting to fall from her eyes.

"Yeah, I'm ok." He was almost passed out. His voice was weak, "Call the office...and... check your waitress friend. She's hurt badly."

Customers in the restaurant were helping Amanda when Sally arrived, so she hadn't noticed that she had been shot, too. She hollered for the cook to call 911 immediately and have them send ambulances and the deputies. The cook ran for the phone as Sally kneeled down next to Amanda. She couldn't believe this was happening. "Amanda, are you all right?"

"I hurt....I hurt so bad....my side...it hurts so bad." A couple of the customers had put some napkins on the wound to keep the blood from running onto the floor, but the paper napkins did a poor job of absorbing all the blood. Sally grabbed a table cloth from the nearest table and wrapped it around Amanda to keep the blood from oozing to the floor. She thanked the customers who had helped and told them not to worry about their tabs... that it was on the house. She also apologized for the situation and asked them to please come back again. The customers were ready to leave when Billy Roy arrived along with two state troopers.

"Ladies and gentlemen, please have a seat until we can get a statement from you," ordered one of the troopers. The customers were not happy to be detained, but followed the trooper's instructions.

As they started taking statements, Sally took another table cloth and wrapped it around Brick. He was still stammering as he tried to speak to Sally.   "How's your friend?"

"She's ok. Oh, Brick. I'm so sorry this all happened. Don't worry, we'll get you taken care of....you're going to be ok....I promise." Sirens were heard in the distance as the ambulances made their way to the restaurant. The attendants came in, loaded Brick and Amanda, and took off for the hospital. Sally made sure that Marie, the cook, at the restaurant would be able to close the restaurant for the rest of the day and evening. Then she followed the ambulances to the hospital.

The coroner arrived just as the ambulances were leaving. He and his assistant examined Roberto. They determined that he died from the gunshot wounds he received in the head and the neck. The coroner met briefly with Billy Roy and the state troopers, after they finished taking statements from the witnesses. The body was removed and everyone left the scene, except Marie, who called in a friend to help her finish cleaning up the mess.

CHAPTER TWENTY-EIGHT

Sally walked into Brick's hospital room carrying a copy of the local newspaper and a couple of candy bars that Brick liked. Brick was sitting up in his bed. She leaned over and gave him a big kiss. "How are you doing today, Sweetheart?" She was staring into his blue eyes and smiling.

"Hi, Honey. I guess I'm doing much better. The doctor said I could probably go home in a day or two. I've been here for a week now, and it's starting to drive me crazy."

"Oh, that's great news, Brick. I'm so ready for you to come home. I miss you so much."

Brick gave her another kiss then asked, "How is your friend Amanda?"

"She's coming along well, and will be discharged in a day or two, as well. I stopped by her room on my way to see you. She asked about you and wanted me to give you this message...getting shot is not the best thing in life, but it's not the worst either...it's what you make of it."

Brick smiled, "Yeah, we're both gonna make it. How's Red? I guess he misses me."

Sally pulled up a chair and sat down reaching for Brick's hand to hold. "Yeah, he does. Dr. Bob has him at the clinic during the day then takes him home at night. He's going to be fine. So, what are you going to do after you get out? Are you still going to be the Sheriff and be in law enforcement? George is back on duty and doing really well. The other deputies have everything under control. Juanita and Bonnie have the office covered....everything is running smoothly. You did a really good job of bringing this team together. I think they would operate real well with a new sheriff."

"Sally, the good people of Maranda and Medina county elected me to be their sheriff, and I'm gonna stay with it and help protect them all. My purpose is to keep the county safe, like it was when we were growing up. Remember?" Sally nodded her head. "No one worried about criminals back then. It was and still is a peaceful, safe place to live, and I want it to remain that way. That's why I'm gonna remain sheriff." He looked into Sally's eyes as he asked the most important question of his life, "Sally, will you still be here beside me, even though I'm going to continue to be the sheriff?"

Tears rolled down her face as she reached over and took his cheeks in the palms of her hands, pressing her lips on his. He put his arms across her back and held her tight...never wanting to let go. "I'll take that as a yes," he said as he kissed her again.

"Oh, Brick...I love you so much. I will always be here at your side. I have dreamed of being your wife ever since we dated in high school. How could I leave you now? You are my one true love, Brick." She gave him another kiss then sat back in her chair. "I can't wait until we start planning our wedding."

"Sally, I can't tell you how much it means to me to have you by my side. I love you with all of my heart." Brick's eyes were tearing up as he continued to look into her eyes. "I want us to get married as soon as we can. Have you thought about when you'd like to have the wedding?"

"Well, first you have to get out of here," she said with a big smile. "Then we can make our formal plans. Maybe in a month or two? I want you to be in good health and feeling your best."

"I do, too! Oh, Sally, you've made me the happiest man alive." He pulled her to him again as the nurse came in with his medicine.

"Oh, I'm so sorry. Should I come back in a minute?" The nurse was embarrassed.

"No," Sally said. "I was just leaving. Go ahead and give him his medicine. We need to get him well soon. He has a promise he's got to keep." She winked at Brick as the nurse gave him his pills.

After the nurse left Brick eased under the bed covers and put his head on the pillow. As he started to drift off to sleep, he wondered why that man wanted to kill him. "Could it have been linked to the drug money Red found?" He fell asleep with this question on his mind.

EPILOGUE

Brick and Sally's wedding took place just prior to Christmas that year. It was a beautiful event shared by many friends and members of the community. Brick wished that his parents had been alive to see the love and joy that was celebrated at the church, not only for the love he and Sally shared, but also for those who attended.

For their honeymoon, they chose to go to Las Vegas. Sally had never been to that area of the country, and Brick wanted to introduce her to Betty and Clem, that sweet couple he met and helped during his short time in Vegas. They were obviously very happy to see Brick again and to meet his new wife. Brick wished they didn't live so far away because he really enjoyed their relationship they had developed.

After their honeymoon, Brick and Sally decided to live at Brick's home. Mom's Garden was so lovely, and Sally enjoyed the wonderful way she felt when she walked through the garden. She learned how to care for the flowers and greenery that grew there.

Charlie, Sally's dog, and Red got along very well, as Charlie got used to his new home. They romped and played all day long in the big back yard. Perhaps it was the incident regarding David that helped the two dogs bond, but whatever it was, they never got in fights or caused problems.

Shortly after Brick and Sally were married, George announced that he and Gloria were expecting a new arrival. They were so happy. It was one of the reasons they moved from Michigan... they wanted to raise their children in Texas. Everyone was so excited for them.

Juanita and Bonnie continued to keep the office running smoothly, while Billy Roy, Albert, Sam and George became more experienced as deputies. The county of Medina was gaining a positive reputation regarding safety and security, because of their efforts.

Brick was very satisfied with every aspect of his life...his wife, his job, his co-workers, and his community. It seemed that he had no need for anything else, and then one day Sally came to him with some news...Brick was about to be a father. What more could he ask for?

CPSIA information can be obtained
at www.ICGtesting.com
Printed in the USA
FSOW02n1622220217
31130FS